LOST AND FOUND FAMILY

A Fantasy & Futuristic Romance Novella

Samantha York

TABLE OF CONTENTS

Book Description

Sometimes it takes decades to find your true family...but only a moment to lose them.

Separated at birth, these twins find they have more than genetics in common: they're both the target of killers who are willing to risk everything to take them out.

Chapter 1: A New Contract

"Hey, did you see that Z posted another contract?" Hugo asked. "Looks like The Killer Queen ripped her off. Claimed she'd taken out that Van der Cleft heir when she really hadn't. Z's contract on her own son is still open, but now she's posting one for a million bucks for that bitch KQ. If both targets are in the same neighborhood, we could make some big bucks fast."

"The boy's worth checking into," Vinny said. "But if you've ever dealt with Zelda Van der Cleft, you'll know you'd better get at least fifty percent upfront. She's a slippery snake when it comes to paying off: ready to bite if you handle her wrong, but also quick to disappear. I don't doubt that there'll be a job out for *her* one of these days. As far as the other, I wouldn't go up against KQ unless I had a death wish!"

"Still," Hugo said, pulling on the edge of his thick black mustache, "there's an island out in the Bahamas that I've had my eye on. If we joined forces, we'd have the bucks to buy it and enough left over for a nice boat to run around in. How about it? I'll let you have the west side and I'll take the east."

"Dummy!" Vinny replied harshly, then snorted.

"Who you callin' a dummy, you peach-faced imbecile!"

"If we're gonna buy an island together," Vinny said in a soothing, gentle tone, immediately trying to calm down the easily excitable assassin, "you take the west side. If a hurricane comes rumbling through, you'll get hit first, not me. A little breeze never seemed to bother you. Don't you ever watch the weather channels?"

"Not if my phone still has a charge. I got a thing going on with that new strip version of solitaire. You wouldn't believe..."

"Hush!" Vinny cut off his protégé's babbling, his hand up to cover Hugo's mouth as he focused on the activity at the store's entrance.

Hugo the Huge didn't have much sense, but he did know

not to cross the short-tempered, short-statured assassin. Stepping aside, he clenched his jaws in suppressed rage and looked over his mentor's shoulder.

"Looks like him to me," Hugo whispered. "How'd you know to look out here in the middle of Nowhere, Oregon for Z's kid?"

"While you were playing those dumb games on your phone, I've been scouting local news stories and obituaries. You'd be surprised how many folks we know who wound up as a John Doe."

Hugo chuckled. "I only know the ones I put on that party list."

"Party list?" Vinny shook his head but didn't comment on the nonsense answer. Hugo was big, mean, and dumb but he was also controllable. He spoke English, but not very well. Still, his hands gripped like a hydraulic vise and — the real bonus — he was born without a conscience. This voice-activated killing machine was just what Vinny needed to get what he wanted in life.

"Are you sure that's him? I thought Van was a skinny crack head. This guy looks like the poster boy for eating organic foods."

Vinny looked down at his phone, opened up to the image of his target. Hugo was right. "Damn! I could have sworn this was the area I tracked Killer Queen's phone signal to."

"Wait!" Hugo said, then pointed to the minivan in the parking lot. "That's him again! How can that be?"

"Well, I'll be bound, tied, and tickled. There really is a twin! Good going, Hugo."

"Hey, since there's two of them, do you think Zelda will pay us twice as much?"

"No," Vinny said, biting off the word 'idiot,' the trigger word that made Hugo go ballistic. "No, I doubt that bitch would part with an extra dime. But watch it calling her by her name. She's Z, all right?"

"Oh, yeah. So, where's KQ? I'm supposed to use her initials, too, huh?"

"I don't know if it makes a difference, but you start calling anything 'killer' other than angry bees, and you'll have cops and environmentalists all over you." Vinny put his phone back in his jacket and pulled out the little quarter-sized tracker. "Stay put. I'll be right back."

The short, sturdy Sicilian sauntered over to the minivan Junior was loading with groceries. "Do you need a hand there, bud?"

Junior looked askance at him. He was at least fifteen years younger than this stranger and fully capable of lifting the recycled dog food grocery bags. "No, thanks. I got this. Thanks anyhow," he said politely, then walked the cart back to the little corral.

Vinny stood by the front tire and watched, quickly squatting down and sticking the tracking device in the wheel well as soon as Van's twin turned away. Then he made a big mistake. He turned to look in the vehicle to verify there really was a twin, hoping to get at least a side view of him.

"Shit!" he whispered as Van stared at him, the eyebrow lift and furrowed forehead focus a subtle indication that he was studying him.

Van's eyes widened as he took a deep breath and held it. *Shit! It's Vinny! I knew Killer Queen didn't have friends but if she bailed on a contract, it's still open. I gotta get out of here!*

Junior walked back to the driver's side of the car, Vinny still standing there bug-eyed, staring at Van. Junior glanced at his brother and saw the same wide eyes and an intense mixture of emotions draining the color from his face.

He may have been born second, but Junior's protective big brother mode kicked in at super strength at seeing the unspoken threat. "If you don't need anything, Sir, I'd appreciate it if you stepped away," Junior said as nonchalantly as he could. "I still have a few more errands to run."

"Oh, yeah. Sure. Sorry. I thought I was seeing double there for a minute," Vinny said, a nervous chuckle escaping as he offered what he hoped was a plausible explanation for the stare-down.

"Yup," Junior said. "Who would have thought it? I just met the guy. We sure do look alike, though, don't we?"

"Just met him?" Vinny squeaked, as he backed away. "Yeah. I'll just run the carts back to the store."

Junior watched as the nervous and now very confused man took a few carts out of the galvanized pipe enclosure and headed to the store, pretending to look like he worked there.

"We're screwed," Van said when Junior got in.

"Maybe," Junior replied, then handed him the tracker. "What do you think we should do with this?"

"You know," Van laughed, "if you weren't already my brother, I'd love you all over again. Are you sure you didn't grow up on the streets? You sure have some strong survival skills."

"Must be hereditary. So, where to?"

Van held up the round metallic disc. "How about we have some fun? Let's drop this off at the sheriff's office. I don't mean him any harm, but if anyone can protect himself, it's O'Reilly. He's a local legend. The cop with a thousand lives...or something like that."

"Okay, let's give it to him, but explain the circumstances so he knows what's going on." Junior watched as another out-of-towner approached the front of the store and stared at them, pointing at their car with a nod and drop-jawed gaze of confusion. "O'Reilly needs to be prepared," Junior added.

"Yeah, well odds are," Van said, squinting to verify his suspicions, "he's already aware of them. Those two stink like East Coast hitmen. I just don't want the sheriff to know they're probably after me. That would open up a whole new bottle of skunky piss from my past."

"Carson?" Junior asked tentatively, then put the car in reverse.

"Yup." Van sighed and shook his head. "I have to tell him. I mean, tell O'Reilly the whole story. I guess you don't know, but Lucy's Uncle Pete was Carson's godfather."

"What?" Junior said and inadvertently stomped on the brakes. "Crap. Does anyone know it was you who killed him?"

"Nope, but I found out that Pete didn't think too highly of him. He actually sounded like he was glad Carson was dead. That was a horrible thing for even me to hear. Maybe Lucy can help me out. She may be Pete's niece, but she's also a pre-law student. Or was. That's all I needed: more guilt. She quit school so she could be with me..."

"Hey! That was her decision. A lot of people get burned out with school or their major just before graduating. Maybe it happened to her, too. Could be that all she needs is a challenging case to get her all fired up. What would be more exciting than getting her fiancé acquitted?"

"You were there, Junior. What do you think my chances are?"

"Pretty good since I was the only witness. All I saw was a man with Harlequin-faced makeup and crazy hair. I'd say that unless you admitted the crime, you got your first 'Get out of jail free' card."

"Well, it wouldn't be my first," Van admitted. "My mother — our mother — bought my way out of a few minor infractions. You know, minor as in getting mad at someone and smashing out the windshield of his Porsche..."

"Ew. Sorry, but when you say, 'our mother,' it sounds so weird. I have two mothers, but neither one birthed me. I'm glad they were excited about adopting you in the family and giving you their — our — name, even if it wasn't legal. You did need a last name, after all."

"Yeah, and since my legal first name is Charles, there shouldn't be any reason Van Wagner is on the government's radar. What a mouthful I had: Charles Van der Cleft the Third."

Junior chuckled as he pulled into the sheriff's department parking lot. "Yeah, I got Junior as a legal first name. Well, at least the name I went through school with. I never did get a social security number. As far as that goes, I'm not a real entity. I'm invisible to the government. My moms didn't even claim me on tax returns as a dependent."

"Cool. The Invisible Twins. Let's hope we can do something about that down the line. In the meantime, I'll take this to the sheriff. Coming with me?"

"Sure, why not. The ice cream is in an insulated bag. We're good for at least an hour."

"Probably more," Van added, "since it's December. Who eats ice cream at Christmastime?"

"Mom," Junior said. "Any time of the year is good for sweets, although she has cut down. Come on. I got your back."

"And I got yours, too. Damn! It's nice having a brother," Van said, his arm around Junior's shoulder. "Better late than never."

***

"So, you say you saw this short, dark-haired man with a clean-shaven face try to sneak this tracker under your wheel well?" O'Reilly asked, turning the high-tech bit over and over, looking for any sign of product identification.

"Oh, he did sneak it in," Junior said. "It's just that I saw him do it in the mirror. What middle-aged man asks a healthy guy in his twenties if he can help him unload his groceries?"

"Maybe he was hitting on you?" O'Reilly asked, hoping he had suppressed his grin.

"Nah. I didn't get that vibe from him," Junior said. "And as soon as he saw Van, he went positively snow white."

The sheriff looked from one brother to the other, then stopped at Van, the one with the guilty look on his face. "Do you know why?"

"I recognized him."

"And..." O'Reilly prompted.

"And he's a hitman."

"Oh."

Van chuckled and shook his head. "I have a past. I never had dealings with him directly, but know of people who did. He could tell I recognized him."

Junior moved in front of Van and took over the conversation. "The man said he was staring because we were twins. I knew he was lying from the minute he opened his mouth, but I let him ramble. I told him Van and I just met. That's the truth, too."

"Well, I'm not an expert," the sheriff said, "but you two look like twins to me. And from what I remember about an incident at the emergency room a couple months ago, you did claim him as your identical twin. Right?"

"Yes, Sir, I did," Junior said. "But what I told that creeper…"

"Vinny the Axe," Van interrupted, then went still again.

"But what I told Vinny the Axe was true, too. Van and I were separated at birth."

The sheriff looked at both of them again and could tell they were telling the truth. "So, what do you want me to do?"

"You can do whatever sheriff-y things you normally do when a hired assassin comes into town," Junior said. "I just don't want him haunting me or my family. When he tagged me – not Van; he saw him after he put the tracker on the car – he was targeting me for something evil. I'm sure you'll agree with my suspicions if you ever meet him. Just make sure you're wearing Kevlar if you do."

"Yeah, well, me and my Kevlar are best of buddies after that she-devil stomped your brother into salsa and shot me at point-blank range." O'Reilly looked at Van and grinned. "You look a whole lot better now than you did. Rumor has it that you've taken a shine to Pete's niece. I'm glad you two are stickin' around to help him out. He's a crotchety old fart, but has a heart of gold."

"Yeah, he does," Van agreed. "Lucy inherited the heart, but thank goodness, she's not ornery like him."

"She's prettier, too," Junior added. "Both of them seem to be good for you, though. We may live in different states, but as long as we're only a CD of tunes away, I'm sure we'll keep popping in for dinner on Sundays. By the way, we're having lasagna this Sunday. Make sure you bring breath mints. Mom loves to put extra garlic on the toast."

Chapter 2: A Research Project

"Damn! Why can't I just look this up on the internet?" Vinny groused to Hugo. His minion was barely literate and wasn't worth a washcloth in a mud bath, but he did have his skills. Too bad he also had the attention span of a fruit fly.

"Huh?" Hugo asked as he shoved his phone into his coat pocket.

"These blasted microfiche are harder than hell to read. Even these glasses the librarian loaned me don't help. Much."

Hugo came and looked over Vinny's shoulder at the blue screen on what looked like an ancient computer. "Micro fishies?" he asked. "I don't see no fishies; just a bunch of words and old pictures."

Vinny silently counted to ten. "No, Hugo. A microfiche is a piece of film. Before they saved everything to a computer, it was printed on paper. Old newspapers and magazines were too bulky to store, so they took pictures and saved the film. They call these films microfiche. I'm trying to use this special viewer to read the microfiche that pertain to newspapers that were out about the time Zelda had her baby. Or babies. I want to know if those two really are twins."

"Didn't the Killer Queen say something about that when you visited her in that Arizona hospital a while back?" Hugo asked, then slipped his phone out of his pocket, ready to play solitaire again.

"Yeah, well, she was so pumped full of drugs and mush-mouthed from brain damage, I wasn't sure if she was hallucinating or just raving mad. I did find out that she sneaked out of that hospital, though." Vinny chuckled to himself. "I guess she found out that I was paying her nurse to report back to me. When I didn't hear back from the old gal for two days, I did a little snooping and found out she was dead. And not a natural death, either."

"Yeah, that foxy KQ never did like bein' spied on, huh, Vinny?"

Vinny rubbed his scarred right hand where she had stabbed him years ago when she caught him watching her shower. "You got that right." He looked over and saw Hugo was sneaking peeks at his phone again. "Go ahead and play your games. I got this." His stomach rumbled, then Hugo's echoed it. "Just give me another half hour, then we can go eat. There's got to be a good Italian restaurant around here somewhere."

Five minutes later, he found what he was looking for. "*Voila!* Look at this." Vinny motioned for Hugo to come see the screen. "See! She only had one. That's her and the old man and the baby: Charles Van der Cleft the Third."

"Yeah, but if I was Van der Cleft's wife, I wouldn't want to share his estate with *two* boys. Shoot! Word was that she bought her way into that marriage. She promised to give him a son in exchange for some stocks or bonds or whatever it is he has that's worth the billions of dollars."

"Hugo, some folks say you're not too bright, but you really come up with some brilliant insight sometimes."

"Is that good?"

Vinny patted him on the shoulder. "Yes, that's very good. At least, it is for me." He squinted to read the rest of the story, continued on the next page. "It says she was delivered by a Dr. Thaddeus Daniels. With a first name like that, he shouldn't be too hard to find."

"Yeah, if he was there, he'd know if she had one or two babies. I think it would be kinda hard to hide having two of them. I know it's pretty obvious when a dog has more than one."

Vinny snapped an image of the article, then put his phone away. "Come on. Let's go eat." He stuck the borrowed reading glasses in his vest pocket. "I think I need these more than that librarian does. She can go buy herself another pair."

***

"Well, that was an interesting conversation," Vinny said, ending the call on his cellphone. He looked up at Hugo. "Ready for another road trip? Looks like we're heading to the old neighborhood back east. That's where Van was born."

"What about his twin? Was he born there, too?" Hugo asked.

Vinny bit his bottom lip, once again suppressing the first words to come to mind with a chomp. "Let's see if there really was a twin first. Then we can see if they were born in the same place."

"Oh! Wait! Duh," Hugo said. "Of course they were. What was I thinking?" He looked back at his phone and grinned. "You're sure missing a lot of hot pictures by not playing strip solitaire, Vinny."

"Just don't start taking off your clothes if you lose. Remember, they can't see if you're really stripping or not. It's just a game with a computer."

"Oh, yeah. I forgot," Hugo said, re-buckling his belt. "So, when do we leave?"

"Right now. The Christmas rush is coming up. Come on. New York, here we come."

"All right!" Hugo said. "I'm ready for some real comfort food. No one makes calzones like Giovanni's."

Bzzz! Bzzz!

"Hey, Vinny. I think that's your phone."

Vinny rolled his eyes at Hugo's declaration of the obvious and answered the call. "Yeah, this is me. Oh, yeah? Really? He's in Portland? What's the name of the street again? Thanks!"

He grinned broadly and turned to Hugo. "I guess real food's going to have to wait. That doc who delivered Z is in state." He opened the app on his phone and typed in the address. "And only six hours away. Take a piss if you need to, and I'll grab some drinks and sandwiches. Time for another road trip."

***

"Is this the place?" Hugo asked, looking up at the high rise from the rolled-down window.

"Yeah, according to the phone call. Let's go find a hotel and get some dinner. It's late. We'll tackle this in the morning."

The next morning, Hugo awoke to Vinny hissing angrily into the phone. "Why didn't you tell me he was dead yesterday when you called? I just drove six hours to get here!"

Hugo knew his boss was getting ready to explode, so he got up quickly. He hurried into the bathroom and closed the door behind him, then turned on the shower to drown out the shouts. Five minutes later, he shut off the water and listened.

"Well, are you done in there or were you just pretending to shower?" Vinny asked.

Hugo stepped out and looked at Vinny, checking for signs of residual anger. "Are you gonna be okay?" he asked.

"Yeah, I was ticked that my contact didn't tell me that Doc Daniels had died last week. I did find out there was an investigation into some improprieties, though. I'll just sneak into his building today, pretending to be an analyst, and see what I can find. You can stay here and order room service. I'll be back later today. You can play your game and even strip if you want to. I'll knock before coming in."

Hugo chuckled. "Yeah, maybe I'll win more if I follow the rules this time." He held his phone up to his face again and grinned. "Ready or not, Lola, here I come!"

Vinny stepped into the bathroom and noticed no towels had been used. Hugo had pretended to bathe again. "And before I get back, would you take a real shower? You're starting to get ripe."

***

"Special Agent Vicenti," Vinny said, flashing his fake ID at the receptionist. "I'll need his log in codes, passwords, and anything else related to those. I'm not concerned with anything current. The improprieties I'm investigating started in December of '91. I'll need access to those records."

The frazzled receptionist pushed the preprinted set of access codes and passwords to yet another investigator. She had long ago decided to accept this as a job and nothing personal. Any feelings for Dr. Thaddeus Daniels had disappeared when he did, three months earlier. At least, he hadn't implicated her in anything. Being the silent mistress who never received anything more than a poke behind closed doors had its merits. She swished an unexpected smile and quickly swallowed it. Invisible for three months, then washed up on an Arabian beach with several important body parts missing: he really pissed someone off this time.

"Thanks," Vinny said, then headed through the door the distracted receptionist indicated. *That was easier than I thought!*

Ten minutes after searching the files by dates, Vinny found what he was looking for. *"Voila!"* He snapped a photo of the data, not wanting to email or save it to any cloud service. He looked innocent enough, but if he did anything but view it, it would raise a flag that it was important to someone.

"Ephraim Heddlestoff, you sly fly on the wall. Looks like I found the source of your start-up money. Let's begin with a phone call, shall we?"

Vinny left the office with a nod, then noticed the receptionist wasn't paying attention to anything but her chipped fingernail. He was in the clear, ready to move forward.

It took a while, but Vinny finally found a payphone in a convenience store parking lot. He dropped in quarters, then placed the call to the corporate towers of the infamous millionaire and entrepreneur, Ephraim Heddlestoff. The hermit had enough innovative ideas to keep ten businesses going. He was aloof, but also human. His weakness for gambling was renown in the underworld. The man would bet on anything. Time to test his theory.

"Yes, this is Doctor Thaddeus Daniels calling for Mr. Heddlestoff. Please tell him this call is urgent. Yes, I'll hold, but only for sixty seconds. I'm sure he'll take the call if you tell him who I am."

Less the thirty seconds later, Ephraim was on the phone. "Thad?" he asked, a squeak of fear in his voice.

"Nope, but close. We have some very influential people in common," Vinny said. "I could explain how I know you and of your relationship to our dear departed doctor playboy, but I'll save us both time and trouble. Who was the one who actually delivered Zelda Van der Cleft?"

"Wha...what are you talking about?" Ephraim asked. "How would I know?"

Vinny laughed notoriously, then said, "Ephraim, Ephraim, Ephraim. You and I both know you can't lie worth a damn. Whether you're holding a pair of threes and betting like you have a royal flush, or you're lying to me over the telephone, it's the same problem. You're headed for trouble. Just tell me who was involved and if there really were twins, and I'll let you live to play the ponies another day. Do we have an understanding?"

Gulp. The audible sound of swallowing in fear came through loud and clear. Vinny had him.

Ephraim looked up at the calendar on the wall and paled. His latest venture was on the rocks and the deadline was approaching. If he disappeared now to protect his own hide, more than just his funds would disappear. Word on the street was Doc Daniels had taken a long time to die. He didn't want to best his old friend's time in the 'How long does it take you to die?' challenge the takedown squads had set up.

"Wagner," Ephraim blurted out. "That was her name. She was the midwife. Doc gave her the runt twin Zelda didn't want. He gave me money to give her so she'd disappear. He didn't want her coming back to him or the Van der Clefts, looking for support money. Plus, they were identical twins. I told her to stay away from the East Coast. Doc didn't want paparazzi to see a kid with the same face as the boy's, and put two and two together. Or one and one. Just the same, she convinced her husband that someone would kidnap their son if they knew what he looked like. The boy was always shuffled off incognito to schools all over the world. He's dead, though."

"Who's dead?" Vinny asked. "Doc?"

"No, I mean, yes. Doc's dead, but my sources said Zelda's all jazzed up about being the sole heir again. The old man is at death's door. Again or still, one of the other."

Vinny huffed in frustration. Another rumor gone wrong. "Give me more about Wagner. How about a first name, address, where she was going. Something."

"I can't remember the first name, but she lived in a high-rise apartment in Flushing near the Expressway. Sorry, I can't remember the address or her first name, but I think it started with a C. Nice lady, middle-aged, average height and weight."

"Grrr," Vinny growled in the phone.

"Sir, I really would like to help you more. Really, I would. But how many midwives named Wagner live in Flushing? Or did in '92. I do remember I went there in a blizzard. I'm positive she moved after I gave her the money..."

Ephraim paused, then smiled. "Sir, I may have something for you. Let me call you back in an hour..."

"Grrr."

"All right, you call me back in an hour. I'm not trying to scam you or run away or anything like that. I just remembered. I have a picture of her for you. I had my little Instamatic and took a photo of her holding the envelope with the check in it. It's somewhere in my cloud storage. It'll just take me a while to research..."

"I'll hold," Vinny said, then groaned as the 'click-click' came through, wanting more coins or a charge card. "On second thought, I'll call you back in ten. You'd better make it snappy."

"Yes, Sir, I will," Ephraim said, multitasking on his phone and his keyboard.

Click!

"Where oh where did I file you?" he asked the computer. "Who says being obsessive about saving everything digitally is a bad thing?"

Eight minutes later, he had it. He opened the file and there she was. "Cecelia Wagner," he said. He pasted the image into a search engine and found her. "Cecelia Wagner of Lakeview, Oregon donates a dozen frozen turkeys for the annual Christmas Event," Ephraim read. "How about that? This article is only a week old. Looks like I get to keep all my body parts intact and on the same continent."

Buzz.

"Sir, the man you were speaking with earlier is on the line again. Shall I tell him..."

"No, no, Liz! Just put him through. And take the rest of the afternoon off."

"Yes, Sir. Thank you!"

Taking a deep, calming breath, Ephraim spoke with a nervous smile in his voice. "I have good news for you, Sir. Not only do I have her name, but I know where she was last week. Cecelia Wagner donated goods to the Lakeview, Oregon Red Cross for their annual Christmas celebration. If you'd like, I can send you the newspaper article and the old picture I took?"

"What in the hell do I want with an old picture? So, that's Cecelia Wagner and Lakeview, Oregon. I don't see why I can't find the same picture by searching it with those words. Thanks for your assistance. Oh, and make sure your receptionist locks her car doors when she leaves. She really is a cutie. It'd be a shame for harm to come to her."

Click!

Ephraim held the phone away from him, looking at the caller ID. Yes, he was definitely calling from a payphone, but the number prefix was local. Gulp. He opened his top desk drawer and lifted off the false cover from his address book, revealing a small handgun. "Nope. Not today. Let's hope not ever. I really have to lay off those cards."

***

"Are you sure these slacks don't make my butt look flat?" Zelda asked her personal assistant, pivoting in front of her three-sided mirror.

The pinch-faced brunette with freckles and horn-rimmed glasses knew not to speak her mind. "Wow!" she said, with feigned enthusiasm. "I wish I could wear clothes like you do."

"So, you think Sixty-eight will like this outfit?"

"How could he not? If he doesn't, he's drunk, blind, or on his way out the door. I have a delectable Sixty-nine on reserve if you're tired of 'Eight.'"

Zelda giggled. "I love it when you call Eight that nickname. On second thought, why don't you ring up Sixty-nine and see if he's amenable to a little getting-to-know-each-other threesome adventure with a new friend? I'll break him in gently. If he isn't up to my standards, I'll keep Eight around for another few weeks. He does know how to tickle a girl's fancy," she said, squirming seductively.

"Sounds like a great plan. I'll call him right now," Friday said with a nod, excusing herself to the privacy of her sanctuary, also called an in-mansion office.

The converted bedroom suite had everything a businesswoman could want: a huge walnut desk, a skyline view, a jacuzzi hot tub with a retractable entertainment system and a comfortable king-sized bed. Her actual workstation — a laptop computer — was lightweight and loaded with the latest technology and programs, ready to be packed into her standby luggage whenever Zelda got the urge to travel. There wasn't a file cabinet in sight: everything she needed was stored digitally.

Although Zelda was a flighty boss and quick to fire those who displeased her, she had kept Friday employed for five years.

That was a longevity record for anyone other than her personal cuisine wizard. Early on, he had discovered that the secret to keeping Zelda happy was his secret 'spice.' No matter what dish he created for her — from soup to eggs to mousse — Cookie topped it with a generous pinch of cocaine. Like everyone else, employees were either assigned a title — such as Friday the personal assistant, Driver the chauffeur — or given a number, like her lovers.

The numbered consorts had started at One, nearly thirty years earlier. When Zelda got to Ninety-nine, she decided to start again with One. After all, One-hundred-and-ninety-nine was such a long moniker to scream out in passion. It was Friday's idea just to use the last number as a name. The male lovers seldom satisfied her tastes for more than a month, and none were memorable enough to recall from the previous year. Zelda was ruthless but efficient.

Friday opened her laptop and checked her Swiss bank account. Yes! Just as he promised, Vinny had deposited the agreed-upon amount. She logged out and opened a search engine. "'Islands for sale Caribbean' ought to work. At least it's a starting point. I can see the writing on the wall. Zelda's face and ass are both sagging. She'll find a way to blame me for both. Maybe Vinny can find a body double for me and knock her off. Death is probably the only way I'd be able to leave on good terms with Z."

Chapter 3: A Botched Break-In

Rural Oregon
December

"Hey, Vinny. Are you sure we're in the right spot? This is the smallest trailer park I ever saw."

"Those aren't trailers, they're RVs."

"Harveys?" Hugo asked, then squinted into his binoculars again.

"Recreational vehicles," Vinny said through clenched teeth. "They're like trailers with motors. When folks don't like the view or the weather, or they just want to get out of town, they simply turn the key and away they go."

"Wow! I think I'd rather have one of those than an island. I can go to the mountains in the summer and beach in the winter. People are pretty smart to live in those." Hugo picked up the binoculars again. "Hey, look. They're all getting into that minivan. I guess they keep a spare in case they wanna go somewhere and don't want to carry their home with 'em like a turtle."

"That's right. And as soon as everyone's gone, we're going in. Time for a little shopping trip."

"What do they have that I need? Hey! Maybe I can just take the whole trailer."

"No, Hugo, we can't do that. Those are easier to track down than a car. Come on. I'm shopping for clues. There's got to be something in there that will tell me where to find Van. Since we know where this twin lives, we can come back here and take care of him whenever. First, I have to get pictures of the two of them together. If Old Man Van der Cleft doesn't know his son's still alive or that Van has a twin, let's hope he'll pay a bigger bounty for two living sons than the contract amount Zelda has for one dead one."

"Gee, you're smart, Vinny. I never would have thought of that."

"Yeah, well, neither did Killer Queen. Still don't know what happened to her."

"I was sure looking forward to squeezing her until she pissed her pants."

Vinny turned to Hugo in surprise and asked, "Huh?"

"She did that to me once. I figure I'd pay her back, and then one-up it. Nobody'd pay nothin' for a living Killer Queen," Hugo said, his voice deep and passionate as he mimed twisting the head off a body.

"Yeah, well, you got that right. Come on. They're out of sight now. Just make sure you wipe your feet before we go in."

"Wow," Hugo said once they were inside. "This looks like a real home..."

"It *is* a real home. For them." Vinny scanned the living room, not knowing what he was looking for, but certain he'd know when he found it. Not finding anything of interest, he headed to the bedrooms in the rear.

Thunk. Vinny stopped at the familiar sound of a refrigerator door shutting, then went to the kitchen to investigate. "Hugo, get out of there! We can eat lunch after I find something good."

"I did find something good. Lookie. It's a chocolate fudge cake. Someone already cut into it, so they won't know if I take just a sliver of it."

Hugo slammed the butcher knife down on the dessert just as Vinny shouted, "No!"

"Wha?" Hugo started to ask, then gasped in pain. Stunned, he looked down and saw the end of his index finger hanging off. Blood spurted like a squeezed ketchup bottle as both he and the cleaver fell to the floor.

"Ah, crap, buddy," Vinny groaned, rushing to his side. He grabbed a dishtowel from the counter and wrapped it around Hugo's hand. "Can you stand up? We gotta get out of here. Shit!

Where's a good cleanup crew when you need one? Hell, we're too far from civilization to get any help on this. It's just you and me, buddy. Hang in there. I'm sure I saw a medical clinic when we pulled into town. I'll get you taken care of first, and then come back. If we're lucky, it'll be a quick couple of stitches for you, and a day or two away for them. That'll be plenty of time to search this place plus sanitize the mess. They'll never know we were here."

"Hey, Vinny? I don't feel too good." Hugo's eyes widened and his cheeks bulged, then he turned aside and puked. "Oh. Now I feel better."

"You could have turned the other way," Vinny said, grabbing a patchwork-quilted placemat from the table to wipe the vomit from his jacket. "Come on. Let me help you up. Let's hope the bear family doesn't come back until Goldilocks can get this mess cleaned up."

"Bears? Goldilocks?" Hugo asked, stumbling to his feet.

"Never mind. Let's go."

***

"Hey!" Vinny hollered, shoving through the emergency room door towards the registration desk. "He needs a doc right away. He almost took a finger off with a knife."

Rosa grimaced and handed the shorter, non-bloodied man the clipboard with paperwork. Before she had a chance to give the standard spiel of, 'Please fill out these forms and return them to me with your ID and insurance cards,' Vinny cut her off and handed back the clipboard. "Yeah, yeah, yeah. I know the drill. I don't have insurance and he *lost* his ID, but I'll pay with a wad of bills that'd choke a hooker."

Rosa's eyes widened with the coarse remark. "Just a moment," she said and went to find a doctor.

"Hey, Doc," she said to the physician at the standup desk.

"What's up, Rosa? You look like you just saw a ghost."

"Worse. A couple of crooks just came in. One's all bloodied. His friend or partner or whatever he is just made a real crude comment about having a lot of cash so he didn't need paperwork. The other one's hand is all wrapped up in a towel. He doesn't look too good. You might want to check on him right away."

"Just give me a sec and let me finish my notes," he said and turned back to the keyboard.

"Doc, I'd really appreciate it if you took care of these guys first. I'm a tough cookie, but those two spooked me."

"All right, but call Sheriff O'Reilly and see if he's around town. Have him drop in. Tell him what's going on. He might know if they're on someone's watch list."

"Good idea. Thanks. I think I'll stay in the ladies' room until you get them settled in a room. The one who isn't hurt scares me!"

He patted her on the shoulder and winked. "I got this."

Dr. Ellington walked into the waiting area and gasped, then quickly composed himself. Rosa wasn't exaggerating. "Looks like your friend needs some help," he said to Vinny. "Come on back with me. I think we'd better get him a wheelchair."

"No!" Hugo groaned in protest, then stumbled forward. "Just let me lie down somewhere."

Vinny positioned himself under the big man's shoulder and asked the doctor, "Which way?"

"Let's use room number three."

"What do you have for pain?" Vinny asked once they were in the room. "I think he's lost a lot of blood, too. Is there a shot or a pill for that?"

The doctor positioned his patient on the bed and was just about to unwrap the towel when he felt the shorter man's breath on his neck. "Give him something for pain first, all right?"

Gooseflesh covered his body with the perceived threat. "Yes, Sir. I can do that. Is he allergic to anything?" Doc asked as he took one step away.

"Yeah," Vinny said sarcastically. "Bullets and blades. Now,

hop to it."

The doctor flung the curtain aside, then half-ran, half-walked to the locked pharmaceutical cabinet. He filled a syringe with the strongest painkiller he had, then decided to add an extra few milliliters, just to make sure the man felt no pain whatsoever. He put the syringe on a tray, covered it, and was back in the room in less than a minute.

"What took you so long," Hugo slurred. "I hurt."

"Not for long," the doctor said. He realized it would cause additional pain to get the man's jacket off. "If you don't mind, I'll just unbutton your shirt so I can get to your shoulder this way."

Hugo flinched, then nodded.

"Just hurry," Vinny said, still holding Hugo's bandaged hand.

The doctor's fingers shook as he moved the dress shirt aside, then warmed up and quit shaking so much once he got to the body temperature yellowed t-shirt underneath. He pulled the collar back with one hand and reached for the syringe with the other. "Almost there..." he said softly, then stretched the cotton knit as far as it would go. His eyes widened at the tattoo, but he didn't say a word. Instead, he kept his head tipped down so neither man could tell that he had seen the 'Kill Count' inscription with multiple hash marks underneath.

"There," he said. "Just give me a minute to toss this. When I get back, you should be feeling no pain."

"Just leave it there on the tray," Vinny said. "You aren't going anywhere until you sew his finger back on."

"Okay," Doc said. He put the tray with the syringe in the sink, then bent down and grabbed a suture kit from the cabinet. "How are you feeling there, bud?" he asked.

Hugo tipped his head up and saw the laceration kit the doctor was opening. "I *fleel* fine," he slurred, then turned away. "Can we go now, Vinny?"

"No, Hugo. We're going to stay here until he gets you all put back together. That shot only works for the pain."

Hugo lay his head back on the pillow and stared at the

ceiling. "It makes you feel good, too. Good enough to sing."

"Oh, please don't," Vinny said, remembering what happened the first and only time Hugo had been drunk. Evidently, the shot he had received was acting on his system the same way. At least there wasn't a karaoke machine in a hospital emergency room.

Dr. Ellington shut out everything but his patient's index finger, quickly and efficiently cleaning the wound and assessing the damage. His battlefield medic skills had taken over. He flinched at the sound of a metal bowl dropping to the tile floor, but continued his ministrations. Finally done with the sewing, knots, and bandaging, he took a deep breath and came out of his self-induced trance.

"Your friend's going to be fine. I suggest you wait here for an hour or so." He looked over at Hugo; passed out, little snorts from his deep sleep escaping. "He won't be able to walk anywhere until the shot wears off. If you give me a minute, I'll get some pills for him. He can take one or two every four hours as needed for pain. When they're gone, good ol' over-the-counter pain meds like aspirin or ibuprofen should work. Don't let him get the sutures wet or dirty. I'll need to take them out in about ten days."

"I know how to take out stitches," Vinny said dryly. "Go ahead and get me the pills. And bring me a few of those syringes pre-loaded with that painkiller. He's a big boy and pills might not be enough for him."

The doctor opened his mouth to protest, then settled into a relieved smile. "I think I can do that. Just give me a minute to find something to put it all in. Be right back."

As soon as the doctor left, Vinny was on his phone. "Hey, Friday. Yeah, we're still here in Oregon. I haven't found anything on the twins, but I'd bet your life that those two guys we saw yesterday were twins. I'm pretty sure by the glare of recognition that the one in the car was Van. I don't care if the other one said they had just met or not: they're twins. Yeah, well, I ran into a snag. Hugo and I were checking out the old midwife's RV, and he got cut doing something stupid. I'm in the ER with him now. He's not feeling any pain, and I'm going to make sure it stays that way. Anyhow, I have to find a place to park him while I go back and do a cleanup. He almost lost his nose picker, but he'll be fine in a week or two. I'll be in touch when I find something concrete. In the meantime, see if you can poke around in the old man's business. See if he's heard whether Van's dead or alive. Go ahead and plant the seed in loverboy Quinn's head that there might have been a twin. Yeah, we work together fine, all right. I still think you need to have an escape plan, though. Zelda's about as vicious as they come, but you know that. You've managed enough of her kill contracts. Thanks."

***

"Rosa!" Jesse called out when he saw her and waved.

She looked at him as if he wasn't there, then headed to the bathroom.

"Wait a sec," he said, then hurriedly pushed his cart in her direction. When he was nearer, he asked, "Are you okay? You don't look so good. I mean, you're still pretty and all…"

Rosa put her hand up to stop her boyfriend's babbling. "Wait out here," she said and walked into the single bathroom.

"What's going on?" he asked through the crack of the door she had intentionally left ajar.

"We got a creeper — or rather, two creepers — in with Doc Ellington," she whispered, then coughed as Jesse spritzed cleanser on the door handle, trying to look like he had a reason for hanging outside the bathroom.

"Sorry 'bout that," he replied, then commenced polishing away germs and fingerprints, just in case anyone was watching him. "Is it something you think I should check out?" he whispered.

"Yeah, if you would. I have a bad feeling about this. And

come back here and let me know when they're gone. Those two really did scare me shitless. I'm glad the bathroom was empty."

"Gotcha. Go ahead and take care of business or whatever. I'll knock three times when the coast is clear." Jesse then sauntered away, humming *La Cucaracha,* listening for clues to where the doc and the creepy men were.

Down the hall, Jesse heard Dr. Ellington say, "I think I can do that. Just give me a minute to find something to put it all in. Be right back." A split second later, the normally mellow physician who generally sauntered rather than walked, was half-running toward the restricted area, a grimace of panic erasing his otherwise handsome features.

"Found 'em," Jesse whispered to himself, then headed to the room the doctor had run away from, one hand on his cart, one hand on the mop handle.

Jesse dry-swabbed the doorway in front of room three, then paused and listened as he pretended to search for something in his supplies. He couldn't hear what was being said nor get any closer than he was, so he knelt down and began worrying an area on the floor with a putty knife, pretending to scrape up chewing gum. Through the closed door, he only caught random words, but they were enough: Van, twins, midwife's RV, kill contracts.

Suddenly it was quiet. Too quiet. The door opened with a swoosh. "What are you doing here?" Vinny growled, his fist clenched as he looked down at the man on hands and knees, scraping the floor.

Jesse looked up and asked, "Eh?" then shrugged his shoulder. *"No comprendo."*

"Well, *comprendo* this," Vinny said. He reached down and grabbed the janitor by the collar. "Scram!"

Wide-eyed with genuine fear, Jesse nodded rapidly. He almost replied in English, then remembered his undercover persona. *"Sí, sí,"* he said, wiggling and squirming his shoulders to escape the crazy man's grip.

Vinny let go and snorted in disgust. "Damned immigrants. Learn English before coming here. No one understands Mexican around here no how."

Jesse quickly squatted to pick up the dropped putty knife and noticed the otherwise well-dressed man's odd choice of footwear. Although he was wearing an expensive dark gray 'Going to court or church' suit, he had on red and white cross trainers, not dress shoes. Jesse stood up awkwardly as his gimpy leg seized up on him, then realized his intimidator was still waiting for him to leave, wordlessly glaring at him in disgust.

Jesse waved goodbye with a nervous smile and said, *"Adios."* He shuffled as fast and far away as possible without leaving his girlfriend behind. It was better to leave Rosa in the sanctuary of the restroom than have her exposed to this guy. She'd been right to stay hidden until he gave her the all-clear sign. She had a toilet and water. She was set to wait this one out.

The only thing he could do now was to contact his former camp and trailer mate, Van. He had to let him know that he and his brother — and probably one or both of the mothers — were in trouble. Big trouble.

Chapter 4: The Investigation

Lakeview Hospital
December 21

"Hey, Jesse. What's going on? And where's Rosa? No one's at the front desk. They're piling up out here. Nothing serious, but..." Sheriff O'Reilly realized that Jesse hadn't responded to any of his questions and was stunned. Or in shock.

"Come sit down a minute," he said, ushering Jesse to a vacant area in the waiting room. He came back to Rosa's desk and addressed the six people anxiously waiting for someone to acknowledge them. "Someone will be out shortly to help you," he said, hoping it was true.

The hospital's director came rushing towards Rosa's empty desk, a strained and anxious smile pasted on his face as he hollered, "I'm coming, I'm coming!" Frustrated people crowded around the desk lit up with phone lines ringing, everyone and everything demanding attention at the same time.

"You got this?" O'Reilly asked.

"I'd better. Where's Rosa?"

"I don't know, but it must be important." The sheriff looked over to the janitor, standing in the corner, holding his phone up as he pivoted in place, trying to catch a stronger signal. "Good luck. Looks like you're gonna need it."

The administrator smiled weakly, then turned to the crowd. "Now, who was next?"

Jesse dialed the call again. "I'll bet he's out at Pete's," he mumbled.

"Who's out at Pete's?" O'Reilly asked, then pulled a chair sideways and sat down, assuming a comfortable position to watch the front door and hallway at the same time. He glanced back at the fidgety janitor standing behind him, worrying his phone. "And what in the hell is going on with you? You're scaring me, Jesse. Nothing but nothing ever spooks you."

"Yeah, well spooks spook me," Jesse replied with a nervous laugh. Seeing that the sheriff had missed his joke, he elaborated. "Spooks, as in hired murderers; they spook me."

"Okay. Where's this spook you're talking about? Is he here?"

"Yeah, but I think there's two of them. Rosa called them creepers. Two guys came in and scared her. Looks like they terrorized Doc Ellington, too. I hope he's okay. He's probably hiding out somewhere, too."

"Give me more, Jesse. And hurry."

"Rosa said two creepers came in and Doc Ellington saw to whatever the medical emergency was. When I saw him, he was running back and forth like he was carrying a live grenade to a bomb disposal unit. At least, that's what it looked like to me. If you think I'm tough to unnerve, Doc makes me look like a Nervous Nelly. He was nicknamed Steely Dan in Afghanistan. He could put GIs back together with just his field kit and electrical tape, even under fire."

"Okay. I get it. These guys spooked you and Doc. You have to give me more than that."

"Well, after Doc left the exam room, I ambled over and listened at the door. I couldn't hear everything that was going on, but I did hear them mention Van, twins, the midwife at the RV and kill contracts. I'm sure they were talking about the guys and Junior's one mom. I know Cecelia was the midwife for Cindy's first kid and will be for this next one, too. Sheriff, I think that whole family is in trouble."

Sheriff O'Reilly's eyes widened at the last revelation. He had done his research after Van and Junior brought him the tracker. Vinny the Axe had a long history of being at the scene of a hit but had never been convicted of anything but assaults and gun possession, and that was when he was a juvenile. The other man the brothers had seen was unnamed and unknown. "Did you happen to hear any names?"

"Yeah. The guy was talking to someone on the phone named Friday about twins and kill contracts. Would you go and check on Doc, please?" Jesse asked. His stomach rumbled loudly and he leaned forward. "Gotta go. I'm gonna be sick now."

O'Reilly headed toward the exam rooms while Jesse went the other direction to the restrooms. "Hey," the sheriff said and nodded to the short, dark-haired man in a classy suit pushing a wheelchair. The passed-out patient with the biggest, thickest black mustache he had ever seen had his right index finger splinted and bandaged, resting on a plastic bag-wrapped basin. "Need a hand?" he asked as he held the door, studying the man's features, then glancing up to make sure the security camera's light was on.

"Thanks," Vinny grumbled, then spun the wheelchair around so he could back out of the facility, his eyes fixed on the sheriff.

O'Reilly grinned and nodded, making sure he kept on his congenial law enforcement officer façade as he watched to see which section of the parking lot they were headed. "Cool," he said under his breath and turned around. Before he went through the automatic doors, he paused at the giant concrete planter. The once vibrant flowering plants were now frozen twigs and bits of desiccated leaves and petals. He pinched off a sprig, brought to his nose and sniffed, continuing to follow the mysterious pair's trek to their rental car — or stolen car — in the window's reflection. He grinned and walked inside, hoping he appeared to have no interest in them. "Very cool. A 1980 Mercury Marquis. That shouldn't be too hard to find."

"There you are!" Jesse said, the fear on his face unmistakable. "Did you find Doc Ellington?"

"I wasn't looking for him. Why? Is he missing?" he joked, then got serious. "Something came up. Come on. Where was he treating the patient?"

"Sorry. He was in room three. Come on," Jesse said, grabbing O'Reilly by the inner elbow and pulling him in that direction.

The sheriff was in the room first. "Oh, Lord," he said, and dropped to the floor beside the doctor, his hand on the medic's chest to make sure he was still breathing.

"Is he okay?" Jesse asked, holding onto the edge of the bed for both physical and emotional support.

O'Reilly turned the doctor's head to the side and saw a syringe still embedded in his neck. He yanked it straight out. "He will be." He reached over and pressed the call button dangling from the side of the bed.

"Can I help you?" the voice asked.

"This is Sheriff O'Reilly. Get another doctor in here stat. I have a man down who just received an injection of an unknown substance. And don't try and call Ellington. He's the one who needs attention."

Rumble. Rumble. Rumble.

The crash cart and nurse were in the room in seconds. "What happened?" she asked, accepting the syringe from the sheriff. She saw the bed was empty, then noticed the body on the floor and quickly knelt down to do an assessment.

"Looks like someone decided Doc needed a break. Is there such a thing as a fatal dose of that stuff?"

"Yes, but not in one syringe, even if... Don't tell me they injected it into his neck."

"Okay, but they did." O'Reilly turned the prone doctor's head towards him so she could get a better look. "I think it would be bleeding, though, if it hit an artery or vein. Looks like the guy didn't know what he was doing. Is that a scrape?"

The nurse leaned forward and looked at the doctor's neck, then lifted up her glasses and inspected the needle. "I'd say there was a little divine intervention here. The needle is bent. He must have hit a muscle. That's why Doc's skin is scraped. Only a little bit made its way in."

"Oh..." Doc Ellington groaned.

"Are you okay?" O'Reilly asked.

"No, but I will be when you let me know you have those

idiots locked up. What happened?" Doc grabbed his belly and groaned. "All I remember is getting punched in the gut, doubling over, then feeling pressure on my back. I think he was kneeling on me."

"Yeah, probably," the nurse said. "He injected this in your neck. Or tried to. Good thing you're tough as saddle leather. What was in this?"

"Morphine. I was going to give the great ape Fentanyl, but I was afraid he'd OD on it. Not the one dose I gave him, though." He paused and coughed. "You see, the little guy wanted additional syringes to use for his buddy when the first injection wore off." The doctor shook his head, trying to clear his brain fog with the physical gesture. "I'll be fine. I won't be able to see any more patients today, though. I gotta find a bed and sleep this crap off. Why anyone would think this is fun is beyond me. Crap."

"Rosa!" Jesse exclaimed suddenly.

"What?" the three in the room asked, looking around for the perpetually perky receptionist.

"She's still locked in the restroom! I gotta go tell her the coast is clear. It is, isn't it, Sheriff?"

"Yeah, both of them took off. Looks like you have this part handled," he said, nodding to the nurse. "Let me go get those guys. Or one guy. The one in the wheelchair didn't look like he could do anyone harm. If I had known about this assault when they were leaving, I could have stopped them right then and there. As you would say, Doc, 'Crap.'"

Just as Jesse got to the door, he paused and turned back. "Hey, wait. You gotta go see if Van's mothers are okay. I tried calling their satellite phone and no answer. I thought it was my phone, but it had lots of bars. Looks like that whole family is in trouble."

"They're out at that new area folks are calling Birds of a Feather, right? Out near Crump Lake?" the sheriff asked for verification, although he already knew where Cecelia lived.

Jesse nodded vigorously, then said, "Hey, I gotta go check on my girl. I'll let you know if I remember anything else."

"You do that," the sheriff called after him, the man's awkward gait exaggerated by his attempt to move quickly without his ever-present janitorial cart/walker.

***

"Dispatch; this is O'Reilly. I'm heading out to the Wagner's place by Crump Lake. I might be out of contact for a bit. I'm not sure if my radio will work out there, but I know for a fact that it's a dead zone for cellphones. If I don't call by noon, send someone out there to check on me. Those two guys I was researching earlier just assaulted Doc Ellington, or at least Vinny the Axe did. Yeah, I'm suited up. Don't worry about me. Unless Vinny has an axe stashed somewhere... Roger that. O'Reilly out."

The sheriff parked in the gravel and made sure he walked on rocks or grassy spots, noticing the recent footprints were as bright as a child's fingerpaint handprint on the wall. He pulled his phone from his pocket and snapped photos of the unusual shoe patterns, then proceeded.

The side door of the RV was still open, a thin tracing of dried blood trailing down the aluminum steps, leading to a gummy puddle of brown dirt-and-blood soup where a car had been parked. By the spacing of the tire treads, it was the same 1980 Mercury Marquis he had seen in the parking lot. Not many of those around. He made a comment into his phone, reminding himself to check on classic cars stolen in the area. The vanity of criminals was often their downfall.

Once inside, it was obvious what had happened. The bloody knife was in the sink, right next to the half-eaten double layer chocolate cake, the smeared letters 'Merry Chri' still visible. "Their vanity and their hunger," he said, snorting in derision.

"What were they looking for..." The sheriff pulled out an evidence baggie, turned it inside out and grasped the knife handle, carefully putting it inside.

Nothing else seemed to have been disturbed. Books, framed photos, and knickknacks were still arranged on the shelves. A basket full of toddler toys was off in the corner, right next to a small playpen containing folded blankets and a homemade picture book. Curiosity aroused, he picked it up. Each fabric page had an ironed-on transfer photo of a different person with their title underneath: Grandma, Nana, Mommy, Daddy, Uncle, Missy, and the last page, Family. "Oh, boy."

The sheriff looked around the living area and searched for items matching the keywords Jesse had heard: Van and twins. There wasn't a picture to be seen of the two men side by side. Except for the one in the baby's book. Mom, dad, uncle, the baby, and grandmas. And the twin brothers, side by side. Earlier, when the brothers had come to his office with the tracker Vinny had placed on his car, Junior said he had told Vinny they had just met.

"Evidence," he said, and put it in a baggie. "If Vinny sneaks back here, I sure don't want him to find this. Time to find 'Family.'"

The sheriff was ready to cordon off the area and leave the mess for the forensic experts to sift through when inspiration hit. A grin of self-righteous satisfaction grew. "Nope. No police tape today. I got the knife. That's all I should need. Nothing else is evidence. Vinny's evaded conviction in the past. He'll be back to get rid of any clues that he was ever around. With all the hubbub here and at the hospital, hopefully, he'll think his buddy already tossed the knife. I will, however, put up one of my dear cousin's little spy cameras."

Sheriff O'Reilly took out the little strip of brushed metal, then looked around the room. The window right across the door had a framed poster above it. 'Bless This Home on Wheels.' He took it down and used the side of his fist to wipe away any dust, peeled the backing off the adhesive strip, and set the thin, wide-angle view camera in place, smack dab in the middle of the copper-colored frame, creating a patterned look. "Yup, anyone walking in will be seen. Thanks for the toy, Arlie. Who could ask for a more generous and creative relative?"

***

"Dispatch, this is Sheriff O'Reilly checking in. All's well at the Wagner's place. Tell me, do you know if Pete ever got a landline put in?"

"No, sir."

"No, you don't know, or no they did not?"

"No, they did not get a landline. I had lunch with Lucy last week. She said there's a backlog on installs. She was hoping to have it before Christmas, so she would have internet and online shopping capabilities, but they told her it wouldn't be until after the first of the year. The only way to contact them is face-to-face or send them a letter."

"I'll take the former. I'm going out there now. Since I'll be incommunicado, make sure my grandson doesn't do anything stupid. I mean, you don't have to *do* anything, just give him 'the look.' You know, the one you give your daughter?"

"Oh, yeah. After rearing her four brothers, I got 'the look' down just right. Anything else? If you want, I can have Butch join us for dinner."

"Great. That'd take a load off my plate."

"Speaking of plates, boss, I'll make one up for you, too."

"Thanks, Charity. Your mom and dad gave you the perfect name. O'Reilly over and out."

***

"Someone's here," Cindy called out. "I think you have a

stalker, Mama."

Cecelia walked to the window, scowling. When she saw it was the sheriff's truck, she smiled as bright as a polished silver Christmas ornament. "Oh! It's Riley!"

"That's O'Reilly," Pete said. "I've known that old coot for years. What's he doing here; bringing me a fruitcake?"

"Pbbt! If he's coming out here, it's probably business. At least, I don't see anything in his hands," Loretta said, then batted her eyelashes at Pete. Again.

Pete returned her gesture with an uncomfortable grin, then turned away and rolled his eyes, suppressing his huff of frustration. *Cute, silly, a great cook, and with the roundest ass in the world. She's everything a man could want in a woman...except she's a lesbian. Why does she keep flirting with me? Is she trying to make me crazy?*

Lady the golden retriever gave her perfunctory 'woof' to announce a visitor, then went back under the table, out of reach of little Missy Lou's fast fingers.

Cindy had the door opened before the sheriff had a chance to knock. "Come on in. It's cold out there."

"Hey, Pete," O'Reilly said, as he stepped in, looking around the room to see how many of the Wagners were there. "Looks like you have a full house."

"Yeah, I do," Pete said. "Ain't it great? It's my birthday dinner. I think you know everyone here, except maybe Cecelia," he added with a wink.

The normally composed sheriff blushed as he looked down at the floor, then over at Cecelia to see if she was sporting a rosy glow, too. She was. "We're acquainted," he said. "I don't mean to intrude on your celebration, but I have a little business I need to conduct."

"All right," Van said. "You can do a little of that 'B' word on one condition: you agree to stay for dinner."

"But...but...it's barely noon," O'Reilly protested, looking up at the clock on the wall.

"Yup. That means you'll have to wait a whole hour and a

half for the turkey to be done," Pete said. "Loretta's making some of her famous cranberry, orange, and apple relish to go with it, too. You can't say no, or I'll let the air out of your tires."

"You know that'd be obstruction of justice," the sheriff said, pouting a feigned frown.

"Yup, and you wouldn't want to arrest a man so close to Christmas, him having all this family around him for the first time, well, ever! Even Jesse and Rosa will be here for dinner."

"All right, but we have to get serious here really quick. Come on, everyone. Sit down, so I can make sure you all hear."

"Okay. Now you're scaring me," Pete said. He settled into his recliner and kicked out the footrest. "Where's that baby? I haven't held her in a whole hour, at least."

Kitchen chairs were used to supplement the sofa and recliner, and the baby set on Pete's lap. "Okay, now we're ready."

"All right, we have a problem," O'Reilly said. "And by that, I mean the Wagners and me."

"Why you?" Pete asked.

"Because I'm sheriff. Just hush a minute and let me finish."

After the giggles died down, O'Reilly continued. "Earlier, Van and Junior came to me with a concern. It seems a couple of hired assassins have been haunting the area. Today, they broke into Loretta and Cecelia's RV."

The room sizzled with gasps that all escaped at the same time. "One of the men cut his finger trying to steal a slice of the chocolate cake he found."

"My cake!" Loretta yelped, then said, "Sorry. Go ahead."

"Vinny — the one Van identified by name — took the wounded man to the hospital. While they were there, Jesse overheard them say something about twins, Wagners, and contracts. I'm pretty sure they weren't talking about movie contracts, either. Oh, yeah. And someone named Friday."

"My birth mother's personal assistant," Van said. "Pbbt. She's as dirty as Vinny the Axe."

"Vinny the *Axe*!" Cecelia squeaked, her voice high with fear, then the others joined in with their concerns.

Panicked comments milled about until O'Reilly hollered, "Hold on! Now look, it's pretty obvious to me that someone wants one or both of you young men gone. I'd say it was you, Van, since you're the new guy in town. Or newer. Plus, I can't see anyone going after a married man who has a little girl and another one on the way. I think we're all involved with this, some more than others. Do you care to enlighten us? It'll make a big difference on how I protect everyone."

"Care to? No, I don't care to," Van said wryly, then chuckled. "But, since I love each and every one of you and don't want to see anyone hurt, here's what I know. My birth mother's name is Zelda."

Van looked at Cecelia. "Only Mama knows what kind of person she really is. She didn't want to split an inheritance, so she gave my twin brother," he nodded to Junior, "away to the midwife." He nodded to Cecelia. "That was great for Junior, rotten for me. Bottom line is our bio-dad has mega bucks — as in, he's a billionaire. A whole lotta good it did him with being a parent, but I digress. Zelda has been waiting for him to die for a long time. He's a lot older than she is and has been in poor health ever since I can remember.

"Personally, I think he's too ornery to die. He hasn't figured out how to turn a profit out of being dead, so he just doesn't cave in to the cancer, diabetes, or whatever the latest malady is. With a living and acknowledged heir — me — Zelda would only get half of his estate. Or less. He keeps the will and trust information pretty close to his bony chest. Whether she gets half of everything or nothing, I don't know. However, the one thing that's pretty certain is that if I'm dead, she'll get everything that was due me."

"Unless your father has named an institution or someone else as his beneficiary," Cecelia said. "Sorry, that sounds crass, but it's true. Now, on the other hand, if your father was to find out there was a twin, you and she would only get half as much. Or a third, depending on whether she's named in the paperwork."

"Bingo!" Van said. "So, I decided it was better to stay low, out of sight and alive, and keep the fact that I have a twin a secret. Two hidden birds that, hopefully, no one will want to throw stones at. I really appreciate having your last name now, too."

"So, what is your last name?" Lucy asked. "I mean, if we're getting married..."

Van reached over and grabbed her hand, then kissed it. "There's no *if* we're getting married, but *when* we get married. I'm keeping the Wagner name. As far as the name Van der Cleft goes, it's a nightmare. If there was a way I could erase all the memories and bad decisions I made..." His bottom lip quivered as he tried to suppress the visions of the crass and violent deeds that were flooding in.

"Honey," Lucy said, "I'm fine with whatever name we want to use. I was just wondering if there was a family name we were going to hand down. Wait! You're Charles Van der Cleft the Third? The missing heir?"

"Guilty. Very guilty."

"Yes," Cecelia said, "but you didn't have any part in receiving that name. You were innocent."

"Yes, but I did have control over what I did wrong later in life," Van said, looking at Junior, then the picture of Carson that was still on the mantel.

Junior stood up and took the handcrafted framed snapshot of Pete and his godson Carson — the man Junior had witnessed Van murder while high — and handed it to Lucy. "Would you put this somewhere for now? We'll talk about it later. Just you and me. Please?"

Lucy looked from Van to Pete, and then back to Junior. "Sure," she said, and put it in the bottom drawer of the end table. "I don't know what's going on with that," Lucy said, "but I agree with Cecelia. A child brought up in hostile situations, without structure or the knowledge of what is right or wrong, is bound to make bad decisions. So, Sheriff, how do we get rid of these bad guys?"

"Ah, that's my niece," Pete said. "Always practical and ready to fix up anything and anybody."

Van gave her a big hug, then a quick kiss. "That's one of the many things I love about her."

The sheriff brought out the plastic bag with Missy Lou's kiddie version of her family album. "Here," he said, handing it to Pete who still held the baby on his lap. "This is the only thing around that I could find without tearing up C's home that shows Junior and Van's relationship; the verification that there really are two of them. Right now, all I can bring against Vinny is breaking and entering. I grabbed the knife the cake snatcher was using when he nearly cut off his finger. I don't think they took anything, though."

"Ew, I feel so violated. Someone breaking into our home," Loretta said.

"Wait. You mean Zelda wants to kill her own son just so she can get more money when her husband dies?" Cecelia asked.

Sheriff O'Reilly subconsciously rubbed the center of his chest where he had been shot months before. "I'd say that's what's going on. I'll bet she's the one who sent the assassin who just about did in both Van and me this summer."

"Killer Queen," Van said softly, then grinned at the memory of her quick but gruesome death, smeared into the asphalt by a semi truck. "At least we don't have to worry about her anymore."

Pete's hands came up around the now dozing baby's head. "What can we do to keep everyone safe?"

"Put the bad guys in jail, right?" Cecelia asked, looking up at O'Reilly.

"Have to have a reason," he said.

Jesse and Rosa had come in during the discussion and were standing by the door, removing their coats and taking in all the concerns. "Right now," Jesse said, "I'll bet the short guy is spending all his time looking after the big one. From what Doc was telling us before we left," he patted Rosa's shoulder, "there's enough pain killer in the pills and syringes he gave him to keep even that three-hundred-pound gorilla dozing for two days. I'd say we have a reprieve."

"Let's hope so. Dinner smells great, my grandson's taken care of for the evening, and I haven't had a chance to relax since..." O'Reilly looked over at Cecelia, unintentionally making her blush with the memory of their afternoon tryst the week before. "Anyways, I think we're all due for a break. It's almost Christmas, so let's make sure we pray for peace on earth, but especially for our little slice of Oregon and Nevada."

"Amen!" Van shouted, a little louder than the others.

Missy Lou started at the noise but stayed asleep.

"Amen," the sheriff repeated.

***

"Hey, Sheriff," Pete said when the two of them were alone on the porch, waiting for Lady to come back from her evening potty break. "What's going on between you and Cecelia? If I didn't know better, I'd say you were sweet on her. Gotta tell you, though, you're wasting your effort."

"Huh? Wasting my... Yes, I'm sweet on her, but why would I be wasting anything on her? She's a charming woman with a wonderful family. She gets a kick out of Butch, too. She says he reminds her of Junior when he was that age."

Pete laughed, then slapped his knee. He leaned back in his rocker and started back and forth. "How can you do that? She's a lesbian! She and Loretta have been together for years. Haven't you noticed Junior and Cindy, and now Van, call her Mama and Loretta, Mom?"

"Yeah, well if she's a lesbian, then I can see Loretta's attraction. Man, can she kiss! No, she's not gay. They're sisters."

"So. Can't sisters be lesbians?" Pete asked, leaning forward, unsure of that possibility.

"I guess they could, but these two aren't. They're together out of necessity. Sort of. At least, Cecelia said it started that way. Her sister was in poor health with diabetes and whatnot, so she stepped in to make sure she was taken care of. Then she got Junior as a newborn. It was easier for them to raise a child together than just Cecelia. Not that Loretta would have let the boy out of her sight.."

O'Reilly's face split into a big grin. "C told me she wasn't romantically interested in any man until she met me. I think it was because she was so busy bringing up Junior, and then becoming a grandma to Missy Lou." He sighed deeply. "But it sure is nice having a gal of my own."

"Are you sure?" Pete asked, looking deep into his friend's face.

"Positive."

"Whoa! Wait!" Pete said as realization hit. "But then that means Loretta's available!"

"Only if she wants to be. But by the way her eyes follow you around everywhere you go, I'd say she was interested in you, too. Do you really think anyone needs as much yard art and planters as those two? Their place looks like a timber craftsman garden of wonders between all the goods you and Van made, and all the birdhouses and bird castles Junior created."

Pete laughed. "Yeah, she does seem to wind up here at least once a week, always with a dish to share, too. Speaking of sharing dishes..." He stood up and whistled for the dog. Lady was there in a flash, tail wagging, tongue hanging out with her big doggy smile. "Let's go in and see how Loretta's doing in the kitchen, shall we? I feel like I just got the key to heaven handed me. All I need is to let her know I'm ready."

"Oh, good grief." O'Reilly stood up to join him. "Show a little restraint, would you? You're an embarrassment to the male sex."

"Sex! Now that's what I'm talking about. It's been a long time, but from what I hear, it's just like riding a bicycle. Just climb on and it all comes back to you."

"Ew! If you approach her like that, you'll lose her before you get to first base. Go gentle into any new relationship. If it doesn't work out, you can always stay friends."

"Friends? Hell, I have enough friends," Pete said. When he saw O'Reilly's scowl of doubt, he amended it. "I have a best friend and a great family. What I'm looking for is a wife!"

"Well, treat her like she's the mare you've been waiting for for twenty years. No hasty movements. They're warm and soft and gorgeous, but can be spooked pretty easy. Shoot! If you do this right, we'll be more than best friends, we'll be in-laws!" O'Reilly clasped his hand on Pete's shoulder. "Come on. Let's go in and see our ladies."

"Ah. Our ladies. That sounds so good."

Chapter 5: Another World, Another Life

Manhattan
December 21

"Quinn? Quinn?" Charles called out, panicked at finding himself alone.

"I'm right here, Dear," the billionaire's personal assistant and lover said, patting the ailing man's hand in assurance. "I just had to take a phone call. Do you need anything? Would you like to try the soup? Zelda said she had Cookie make some up special for you."

"That bitch and her coke-head cook. If either one of them has touched it, I don't want any. Just grab me one of those frozen dinners. At least I know if it came from the market in a sealed container, it's safe."

"And if I'm the one preparing it," Quinn added.

Charles chuckled in recall, then started to cough. "Yeah, he couldn't scoot out of here fast enough. Didn't even stop to grab his coat. I'll bet he about froze stiff before he got to the subway. What was his name?"

Now it was Quinn's turn to chuckle. "Who cares? I'll make sure no one hurts you, my dear." He bent and kissed Charles on the forehead, then pulled back and watched the worry and pain lines fade from his lover's face. "Thank you for living so long," he said tenderly.

"Why do you do this for me? Is it because you won't have a job when I die?" Charles asked, worry creeping back.

"No, you know that's not it. You've set me up with enough shares and cash that I'll never have to work again. You know I do it out of love. And you know what?" he said, then bent to kiss him gently on the lips.

"Hmm?" Charles asked wordlessly, at peace again.

"I don't consider this work. Every minute I get to spend with you is a treasure." Quinn pulled his chair closer to the modified hospital bed and lay his head next to Charles's hand. "Touch me?" he asked.

Charles lifted his hand and set it on Quinn and gently stroked his graying temple. "You have such thick, beautiful hair."

"I think it grows like that just to satisfy you. You do know that it grows faster on the side you can reach. Maybe I should turn over so you could get to the other side, but then I wouldn't be able to see your smile."

"What did I ever do to deserve you?" Charles asked. "I've been a horrible person. Yes, I've neglected my wife, but she doesn't seem to care. She has her string of lovers to keep her happy. You know, once upon a time, I actually liked having sex with her..."

Charles could feel Quinn tense at the admission, so he changed the subject of his melancholy reflection. "I guess what I regret the most is not spending time with my son. Looking back, I remember seeing the hope in his eyes when I came out for a photo shoot or dinner or to make a donation to the school he was going to attend."

Charles's voice suddenly had a smile in it. "Did you know that kid got kicked out of so many private schools, my last resort was a monastery? Even they wouldn't take him! And I was willing to build them a new chapel, too!"

"He probably just wanted your attention. I know that's how I was when I was younger. I had a great mother, most of the time, but when she'd bring home a new boyfriend, it all came tumbling down. She didn't have time for me. The men resented even the slightest attention she'd show me. So, I left home early, developed a skill set working with an outreach program for street kids, and the next thing you know, I'm here."

"Quinn, your attention to detail is what got you in the door. Your creative bargaining ideas that allowed me to, shall we say, bake my cake and eat it, too, brought you to the top. You earned your position in the business, but won my heart with just being you. No skill set required."

"What are we going to do? You can't die on me," Quinn said, feeling the last bit of Charles's vibrancy slip away, a chill sweeping over the two of them, snuggled as close as tubes and monitors would allow.

"Find my son. Ask him to forgive me, would you?"

Quinn sat up and kissed Charles's hand. "How about you get better and we'll do it together? I know you have more than one spark left. And if you feel it start to fade, I'll jump start you with a few of mine. Deal?"

Charles coughed and chuckled at the same time. "Are you going to hire an ambulance to drive me all over the country? I've had people looking for him everywhere for over a year now. If he's alive, he doesn't want to be found."

"Let me try a different tactic. You have to pull yourself together, though. I'd do it for you — you know that — but *you* need to do it for you. Come on, sit up, suck in the new year. Daylight hours are getting longer now. There's more energy in the cosmos. Grab your share, and while you're at it, grab Zelda's. She's already hogged too much of your life energy."

"Yeah, well, she's going to have a shock coming when I do die," Charles sighed, then turned away.

"Hey," Quinn said. "Not until you find Van. Who knows, maybe he has a kidney he's willing to donate."

"Yeah, well, some things money can't buy, I guess. Damned unique tissue."

***

"Hey, Friday, this is Quinn. No, he's getting better, much stronger today than yesterday," he lied. "Oh, and tell Zelda thanks for having Cookie make that soup. He said it was delicious. So, I was just wondering; now that the old man is feeling chipper, he's asking about his son. You did say you had some private investigators looking for him, too. Any leads? No? Dang. He said he was going to give a million-dollar bonus to the first one who gives him proof that his son's alive. I gotta tell you confidentially, though, if he saw the kid before Christmas, I'm sure he'd triple that amount. Or at least, I'd make sure he — or she — got a more than generous bonus for bringing him in to see his dad. Yeah, I know it'd be tough to meet that deadline; Christmas is only a few days away. A New Year's gift and mega bonus would be just as great, though. All right. Make sure you keep me in the loop. The old man and I are flying out of the country to check out the holiday lights in a few of the bigger cities around the world. I'm not sure where we'll wind up, but you have my number. I'd love for you to be the one to get that big fat bonus. *Ciao*, baby."

Quinn ended the call, then gagged in disgust and wiped his mouth with the back of his hand.

"What's wrong," Charles asked.

"Oh, I thought you were still asleep. I was just kissing up to Friday. It always leaves a nasty taste in my mouth. She's still Zelda's brains, or reins, depending on how ambitious the woman-who-shares-your-name is."

"Thanks for not calling her my wife. How about a little physical therapy?"

"As much as I'd like to, I don't think you're ready for that yet," Quinn said, remembering their 'therapy sessions' when they first got together ten years ago.

"You give me too much credit," Charles said, straining to sit up. "The desire's still there, but the body needs to get stronger first. Come over here and help me sit up. If we keep at it, I'll be able to walk to the bathroom by myself in a day or two."

"Yes, dear, but let's take it slowly. And I'll send out for some bagged salad, too. Maybe it's time to listen to the nutritionist and eat more fresh fruit and veggies."

"If it's a choice between spinach and funeral services, I think I'll go for the greens."

Quinn put his arm behind Charles's back and helped him sit up. "Great decision, Popeye," he said and kissed him on the top of the head.

***

"Change of plans," Friday said into her phone. "The price just went up. Van's worth more alive than dead. Plus, if you bring in that twin, I'm sure there'd be a bonus. No, it's the old man, not Z, who's paying this time. Speaking of Zelda, she's getting on my last nerve. I'm ready to split the country. I just want a few extra euros in my account first. But, the bounty's still good on Killer Queen. Z's still ticked at her. Bring her in, and we'll have the classiest little getaway in the Islands. What? I'll tell you why you should split it with me. Because if I wasn't feeding you — and only you — first-class intel, you'd still be chopping off body parts for bookies in The Bronx. Yeah, you, too. Later."

Vinny ended the call, then climbed the outside stairs to the second floor of the one-star hotel, letting himself in with an archaic metal key. "Who doesn't use key cards?" he asked, fumbling with the metal key, trying to figure out which side was up.

"Hey, Hugo!" he called out, not caring if he disturbed anyone else in the hellish hotel located in the middle of Nowhere Nevada. "Are you ever gonna wake up?"

"Huh?" his wounded partner mumbled, slobber dripping from the side of his mouth as he lifted his head from the pillow.

"No more pills, okay?" Vinny said. "You gotta get out of this funk. It's been three days. I hate this no man's land. Not a decent place to eat. I'm sick and tired of hamburgers and milkshakes."

"Milkshakes?" Hugo slurred, a crooked smile rising at the prospect of food. "Can you get me a double chocolate malt with those little candies crushed up in it? What do they call it?"

"Garbage is what it is," Vinny said. "Let me see your hand."

Hugo let him take his hand, then flinched. "I want another shot. I hurt."

"No more shots. Even if I had any more, I wouldn't give you one."

"How about pills? Do we have any of those left?"

"No," Vinny grumbled, then allowed a growl to escape. "You downed the whole bottle day before yesterday. I thought you were going to die. You almost stopped breathing."

"But I hurt," Hugo whined. "Make the pain go away, pretty please."

"Have you been drinking?"

Hugo looked embarrassed and wouldn't meet Vinny's accusing gaze. "Well, maybe. Just a little bit."

"How? Shit! You called room service when I was out getting dinner, didn't you?"

"They don't have room service here," Hugo said, "but I told the kid at the front desk that I'd give him a hundred bucks for a bottle of fine whiskey. It wasn't very fine — it made me cough and burned my throat — but it did the trick. Can I have some more?"

"No," Vinny huffed, biting off the word idiot before it slipped out. "And *all* whiskey burns on the way down, whether it's good or bad. Now, brace yourself. I'm gonna take off this bandage and look at the stitches.

Hugo's head flopped back on the pillow, the combination of a hangover and infection stealing all his energy.

"Damn!" Vinny said, then gagged. He hastily rewrapped the wound. "Change of plans. Your hand needs a bath. A very hot bath. Do you smell that stink?"

Hugo sniffed, then started coughing. "Smells like a shit took a shit."

"Yeah, well you got that right. Stay put. I'll get you something else to drink. Maybe tequila will go down a little easier. Better still, I'll see if I can make you some of my granny's pain-free punch. Don't go anywhere. I'll be back in a flash."

Ten minutes later, Vinny was back from the liquor store.

He grabbed the two glass tumblers the hotel provided, rinsed them out, then poured grain alcohol to the half-way point of both. He opened the bottle of what he called Mad Dog, took a hearty swig, then topped off both glasses.

"Hey, Hugo." He set one glass down and shoved the dozing man's shoulder to rouse him. "Hey. I got you some of my granny's punch. Try some, then I'll get that stinky hand of yours cleaned up."

Hugo's red eyes blinked open. He looked around, momentarily confused about his surroundings, then elbowed his way up to a sitting position. "Does it taste good?" he asked.

"Very good," Vinny said, bringing the cup to his own nose and inhaling. "Almost too good," he added, fighting back the temptation to down it himself.

"Okay. I'll try it." Hugo took a sip, then decided it tasted great and chugged the rest. "Got any more?"

"Yeah, here. Just this one, though."

Hugo downed it in three, quick swallows. He slammed the glass onto the lamp table, hitting the edge of it, nearly sending the tumbler to the floor. "More."

"No. Let me go fill the sink with hot water, soap, and a little booze. That ought to clean up your stinky cut."

"Will it hurt?" Hugo whined.

"Not so much now that you've had two cups of Granny's punch. If I don't do something, though, you'll lose the end of that finger."

Two minutes later

"Hey, Vinny, I'm sorry. I really didn't mean to hit you. It was reflex. Are you gonna be okay?"

Vinny kept the hand towel pressed to his nose. He tipped his head back, then leaned to the side and spat blood that had run down the back of his throat into the toilet. "One, two, three..."

"Why are you counting?" Hugo asked, his left hand still soaking in the sink.

"Because if I get to fifty and you're still standing there, I'm gonna shoot you!"

Hugo looked around Vinny to see whether his gun was in his holster or not — it wasn't — then started to falter. "Whoa! I'm dizzy. Is that supposed to happen when you get a defection?"

"That's an infection, and the reason you're dizzy is because you're drunk." Vinny removed the towel then looked in the mirror. "Damn! I'm gonna have two black eyes."

"You can wear sunglasses and no one will notice. That's what my ma used to do."

***

Tink! Tink! Tink!

Quinn looked down at his phone, verifying the personalized ring tone: it was Friday.

"Hey, Doll," he said brightly, then stuck out his tongue and grimaced. He looked at Charles, sitting upright, biting into a broccoli spear, and an instant smile bloomed. His lover was taking care of himself for the first time since he'd known him. *It's a start. A late one, but still a start.*

"Oh, I'm sorry. I missed that. Damned stifled sneeze," he lied. "You were saying? Really? Laketown? Oh, Lakeview. Let me write that down. Do you have an address? Yeah, well, let's hope you're right and everyone *does* know everyone else in a small town. Okay. If he's there, I'll get you taken care of. Same routing info? Yeah, I have it on file. I'll be in touch. *Ciao.*"

"I take it by that initial scowl and your special one-word dismissal that you were talking to Friday," Charles said, smiling at Quinn's apparent discomfort. *Yes, he'd do anything for me. Such a treasure.*

Quinn lifted Charles's hand and kissed it, then sat down on the bed beside him. "Great news! She told me where Van is! Not an address, per se, but it's a small town in Oregon near the Nevada border. I'll fly in, rent a car, and see if I can have him back here by Christmas morning."

"No," Charles said flatly, shoulders back, frowning. Defiant.

"What?" Quinn gasped. "I thought you wanted to see him."

Charles's frown morphed into the brightest smile Quinn had seen in years. "I'm going with you. I don't want to wait for his return trip. Besides, getting out of this place will be good for me. Who knows? Maybe I'm allergic to high rise buildings."

Quinn brought up his phone. "I'm on it! Finish up that green smoothie, then we can get you spruced up in your best."

"No," Charles said, using the same contrary tone. He caught Quinn's eye and winked. "I'm going casual if we're heading out West. How about something comfortable, like my workout clothes?"

"Better yet," Quinn suggested, "how about that jogging suit I got you? Wind resistant and tailored perfectly to show off your broad shoulders and long legs."

"I feel stronger already." He tipped up and finished his super greens drink. "Doesn't taste as bad as it looks."

Quinn chuckled. "That'd be hard to do. I drink mine out of an opaque glass. Can't stand the sight of it. I'll do that for you next time, too. Come on. We have a family reunion to go to." *I hope.*

***

"Good afternoon, Sir," Quinn said to the hardware store clerk. "I'm looking for a man..." He reached into his vest pocket to retrieve the picture.

"Of course you are," the grizzled man said. "Aren't we all? No, sorry, that was rude. Good help is hard to find; a handyman even more of a challenge."

"No, Sir, not a handyman," Quinn said, smiling weakly. "I'm sorry I don't have a more recent picture, but I was told my friend's son was in this area recently. They haven't seen each other in a long time. My friend's in poor health..."

"Say no more," Clerk said, taking the photo from his hand. He turned the high-quality portrait over, looking for a date. "How old is this?"

"I'm not sure. The young man would be twenty-seven now. Or rather, he will be in a few days."

"Shoot! This is Van! He lives across the state line in Nevada. He's been helping Pete since last summer, I think. Nice kid. Last I heard, he and Miss Lucy were getting hitched."

"He's engaged!" Quinn exclaimed. "His father is going to be so excited. Can you give me an address? We'd like to see him before Christmas."

"Hmm..." The clerk pulled out the drawer under the counter and started rummaging. "I have a map in here somewhere..."

Ding! Ding!

The clerk looked up at the young man in a full-body snowsuit walking in. Quinn stepped to the side and pawed through the discounted tool bin, trying to be unobtrusive.

"Hey, Butch! What's going on?"

"Oh, I was out trying to make a few last-minute bucks, packing firewood or whatnot, so I could get Grandpa a gift for Christmas. I'm on my way out there to Pete's for the big dinner now," he said, patting his weather protection. "It's a little brisk, but I like being able to go where I want on my own two wheels. Hey, do you think you could let me have that cordless chainsaw on a payment plan? I'd like to take it with me now."

"You haven't bought him a gift yet?" the clerk asked, forehead furrowed and lips pursed, ready to scold him, but holding off because someone else was in the store.

"Excuse me," Quinn said. "By any chance, is this the same Pete where Van lives?"

"Oh, yeah," the clerk said, smiling at the good fortune and shutting the drawer, giving up on his search for the map.

Butch agreed, "Sure is."

"Grab your grandpa's gift and let's going," Quinn said, pulling an envelope out of his down-filled jacket. You're my navigator. We're going to Pete's." He handed the clerk five one-hundred-dollar bills. "Is this enough?"

"Sure is. I'll just keep the balance here on account," he said, then looked at Butch. "On account you don't know how to handle money worth a darn. You'd have this eaten up in burgers and fries by the end of the year if you had your way."

The boy shrugged and grinned with sheepish guilt. "Watch my bike for me, will you, Les?" Butch asked, taking the lanyard with the ignition key from around his neck.

"Yeah, yeah. I'll lock it up in back. Be careful out there. It might not be in the forecast, but my rheumatism says there's a big storm on the way."

"Don't worry," Quinn said. "I made sure the rental had four-wheel-drive and the biggest emergency kit available."

"Hey! What's your name?" Les asked, suddenly panicked that his friend's grandson was taking off with a stranger.

"Quinn," he said. "Here, you might want to have this," handing him a business card. "Please, don't let Pete or Grandpa or anyone else know we're on the way. Van's father wants it to be a surprise."

"Well, okay. But I'm calling out there in three hours. It should take you less than two to get there, barring any weather or road problems. And just so you know, I have security cameras and know what you look like. And besides, his grandpa's the sheriff. You don't want to mess with O'Reilly, even on a day when he's in a good mood!"

"Not a problem," Quinn said. "I'll tell him you were looking out for him."

Les straightened up the counter and went for the broom after the two had left. "Shit!" he said. He looked out and saw taillights leaving. "Pete doesn't have a phone! I can't call him. What have I done?"

***

"Butch, as I said, I'm Quinn. I'm assisting my friend Charles in finding his son, Van."

"Van has a dad? I thought he only had two moms."

Before Quinn could reply, Charles moaned in his sleep. Quinn had set up an impromptu bed with oversized pillows, plush blankets, and sleeping bags, making him as comfortable as he could with items taken from the personal jet and bought at the sporting goods store.

"Can we wait for questions or comments later. Charles is in poor health. This trip has been rough on him. I'd like him to get some sleep on the way there. Just tell me directions. I'm sure all will be revealed when we get there." *Or not. Let's hope for not revealed. This is going to be hard to keep out of the papers and off Zelda's radar.*

Chapter 6: Up on the Rooftop

Christmas Eve
Pete's Place

"It's getting warmer, not colder," Jesse said, looking up at the clear sky. "It's going to snow."

"Pbbt! There wasn't anything in the paper today about snow," Pete said, rocking in his old reliable porch chair.

"Yeah, well maybe not, but you don't get the paper until it's a day old. I've been living rough long enough to know when a storm front's coming in."

"Well, if that's the case, then we'll have to bring out the air mattresses and quilts and have a giant slumber party, because I'm not telling anyone what you said. This is the first decent Christmas Eve I've had in twenty years. I'm not gonna let some white fluffy stuff — or the chance of it — ruin the first Christmas party I've ever had in this house. The ham's in the oven, yeast rolls are rising, and all the bookcases are topped with casseroles waiting their turn in the oven or pies cooling off. I've never smelled anything so delicious in my life."

Jesse chuckled. "Sounds good to me. I bought myself a new sleeping bag and brought it with me, just in case. It's a double-sized one."

"Does Rosa know you'll be sharing with someone?" Pete joked.

Jesse slapped him on the shoulder. "Are you kidding? She's the one who picked it out!"

***

"Van," Lucy said softly, sneaking up behind him and giving him a kiss on the neck under his ear, his sensitive spot.

"You know what that does to me," he murmured, turning to face her. "You have my complete attention. What can I do for you?"

"You are so accommodating," she giggled, then quickly and discretely kissed him on the mouth. "Come with me to my room for a minute. I have an early Christmas gift for you."

"Here? Now? With so many people in the house?"

"No, not that silly. Still, it would be nice..." Lucy sighed, trying not to get distracted. "Humor me, all right?"

"Yes, Dear," he said, and pulled her close, a support for her gait just in case her legs 'spazzed out' again.

Once they were in the room, he sat on her bed and asked, "What's going on?"

Lucy reached into the drawer of her nightstand. "Here. Look."

Van took the large manila envelope and opened the clasp. "Fancy wrapping paper," he mocked.

She slapped him playfully on the shoulder, then sat on the bed next to him. She held her breath, waiting for him to take the papers out, then let it out all at once. "Here," she said, taking the envelope from him, exasperated at his hesitancy. She reached inside and pulled out the three-sheet packet. "Look! You're clear. There never have been and never will be any charges against you for shooting Carson. Scratch that. No charges against anyone who may or may not have allegedly shot Carson. No one's pressing charges, no open case. The only witness was Junior, and he swore out an affidavit that even if he met the man — if it even was a man — face-to-face, he wouldn't recognize him."

"But, what about..."

"What about what? Carson's parents could, but didn't, seek out the shooter. The police department is overloaded with unsolved cases, and the coroner's report said that even though he died from a gunshot wound, his heart was such a mess between physiological issues and scar tissue that it was a miracle he even lived as long as he did. You don't have that nasty skeleton in your closet!"

"But how do you know about all this? I was going to tell you, but couldn't work up the nerve. This was the nasty in my life that was keeping me from marrying you."

"I had a talk with Junior," Lucy said, snuggling up under Van's shoulder, "then I spoke with Uncle Pete, and you know what? Everyone dies. Yes, you didn't have the right to take his life sooner than later. Junior did say it was less than a minute from 'the incident' until he was dead. It was an accidental act of mercy on your part. I think I know you well enough now to know you won't be 'helping' anyone else in that direction, right?"

Tears were streaming down Van's cheeks. "Right, very right." He held her close, then kissed her. "This is the best Christmas gift you could have given me."

"Yeah, well it gets better," she said, pulling away. "Van Wagner, you may have been born first, but Junior's already two ahead of you in the progeny department, so congratulations! You're going to be a father!"

The muscles holding up Van's neck suddenly liquified, and he slumped sideways.

"Whoa, there, fella," Lucy said, holding his head close to her bosom. "Take slow, deep breaths. It's going to be okay. Not that I thought you were going to cancel on marrying me, but now you have two good reasons to make it legal: no skeletons in the closet and impending paternity."

Color and strength returned to Van with the deep breathing. "Lucy, you don't need to be pregnant to marry me. I mean, you don't need to be pregnant for me to marry you. I mean, I'd want to marry you even if we never could have children. Look at Loretta and Cecelia. Adoption worked great for them. Bio babies aren't necessary for a great relationship. I don't even want to go there with how my..."

"Then don't," Lucy said. "Come on. A simple wink will let

Junior know that we've had the conversation. Oh, and only Cindy and Cecelia know about the pregnancy, and that was out of necessity and confirmation and all that jazz. I'll let you announce it to the others at dinner."

"Hmm. I guess I'll see if Pete will let me add to his Christmas blessing tonight."

"You do that," Lucy said, squeezing him again. "It's hard to believe you're the same man I met less than a year ago, Burt the chimneysweep."

"Funny," he joked, "you're just as sassy as ever."

"Yup, that's me: your sweet and sassy sweetheart."

"And I'm the unforgettable lover you thought you'd never find."

"I don't believe in accidents," Lucy said, pulling open the bedroom door. "I say, we were meant to be together."

"I'll second that assumption," Van said, then looked up and paled at the man Pete had just let in. "Quinn?"

"Hey, Van. How's it going? You're looking good," Quinn said, a mixture of happiness and surprise on his face. "Very good."

"Who's this?" Junior asked, stepping toward the opened front door to see who had stunned his brother.

Quinn looked from Junior to Van and back again, then fainted.

Junior reacted quickly and caught him before his head hit the floor.

Van started laughing and couldn't stop. Whether it was from nerves at seeing the normally composed Adonis laid out or relief that his whereabouts were finally known, he wasn't sure. "Come on, big guy," he said, stooping beside his father's long-time personal assistant and probable lover. "I didn't faint the first time I saw him, but I was chemically compromised and pretty much out of it. Lucy, someone; would you get me a cool cloth and a glass of water?"

"But who? What?" Quinn asked, looking from one to the other while finding his way into a seated position.

"Zelda's pretty good at keeping secrets," Van said.

"How do you tell each other apart?"

"Oh, that's easy," Junior said. "If he looks like me and isn't a reflection, then it's Van."

"Or, as I say, I'm the handsome one," Van quipped.

"Used to be he was the skinny one," Junior added. "But then he started hanging around Lucy and filled out just fine." Junior stood shoulder to shoulder with his brother and nodded at Quinn. He asked softly, "I take it he's a friendly?"

"Lord, I hope so," Van whispered, then spoke up. "You're not out to kill one or both of us, are you, Quinn?"

"What? Oh, shoot. No. I made a few calls — or rather one call to Friday — and said there was a new bounty out on you, but only alive, not dead. Your father is waiting in the car. He's not doing so well, and wanted to see you."

Van slumped to the couch and bent forward, words and emotions put on hold. "And Zelda?"

"Who knows. She has her stable full of studs, eager to be the recipient of her affections and baubles. I did hear from the maid something about Killer Queen being the only one with an axe to grind to worry about."

Junior and Van looked at each other and smirked. "No worries about the highway streak," Van said. "She tried but didn't get me. Or at least she tried, but I survived."

Sheriff O'Reilly and the others had been sitting or standing at different spots in the living room/dining room area, watching the family drama unfold like a dinner theater production in front of them. The sheriff spoke up. "She tried to get me, too," he said. "But, don't worry about her. She's gone. Yeah, Van and I are tougher than we look."

"And Junior, too," Cindy said. "Since he's Van's twin, that automatically makes him tough looking, too. Actually, though, I think he's kinda cute."

"They're both cute," Cecelia said, coming over to put her arms around both of them. "Now, where is Mr. Van der Cleft? I haven't seen him since..." She looked from one twin to the other. "Since you two were less than six pounds each."

"You? Who are you?" Quinn asked.

"I'm the midwife who delivered Zelda of these two fine young men. And I had the honor of rearing Junior as my own. Oh, and as of about six months ago, I am also Van's mother. Officially, well, maybe not, but we claim each other."

"Morally and emotionally, she definitely is," Van said. "Just to be clear, no animosity toward my father, but I have chosen my family. If it helps him heal, yes, I'll see him. But no, I don't want any part of the family business or the money. And I certainly don't want anything to do with Zelda! She's the one who put a contract out on me and Junior."

"What? It was *Zelda* who put out the contract to murder you? And she knows about Junior?" Quinn asked, then shook his head in confusion. "Of course, she knows about him. She was there when he was born. She was awake at the time, right?"

"Oh, very much awake," Cecelia said. "She...

Clunk. Clunk. Clunk.

Junior went to the door to help whoever was trying to get in.

"Hey," Butch said, his shoulder under the tall, gaunt and ashen man. "Can someone help me get him to a chair. He wouldn't wait in the car any longer. I tried to stop him, but he's one stubborn man."

"Not stubborn," Charles hissed into his chest, then picked up his head and said resolutely. "Determined." He saw the familiar face and reached out to Junior. "Van!"

"Um..." Junior said, then took over supporting the frail man from Butch. "Hello?"

"What? Are you all right?" Charles shook his head in confusion. "You look like Van, but you're not Van, are you?" He didn't wait for an answer before calling for help, "Quinn?"

Quinn rushed over and took Charles from Junior. "Let's sit down. Here's a nice recliner."

"That's my recliner," Pete whispered, then Loretta elbowed him in the ribs. "Help yourself," he said louder. "Care for a drink? We have cider, coffee, eggnog, and a little wine around here somewhere.

"Can I have a soda?" Butch asked, then saw his grandfather the sheriff scowl. "Water would be fine for me," the teen amended.

Charles looked from one twin to the other. "Two?"

"Yeah," Quinn said caustically, "I guess there's a lot more that Zelda's been hiding from you. Evidently she put out a contract on Van. Greedy bitch," he added under his breath.

Charles could tell by the looks on their faces — one embarrassed and ashamed; the other oblivious and confused — which was the son he had intentionally ignored since the moment he was born. "I'm so sorry, Van. Can you ever forgive me for not being there for you?"

A menu of emotions transitioned across Van's face as he recalled all the situations he had endured as a child and teen: all the scores of fixes he had employed to compensate for the lack of love from both parents, then all the horrible deeds he'd done to lash out at the world he felt had wronged him. If he could be forgiven for even one of them by forgiving his father for the one pain that hurt the most — neglect — then he would.

And then it hit him. He *had* just been forgiven. Less than ten minutes ago, he had been exonerated of murder. Freed from that prosecution not just by the overburdened police department, but by the parents and godparent of the young man he had shot; by the brother who had seen him do it and not sought vengeance. A year ago, he had also been pardoned by his brother's wife, Cindy, an innocent he had raped before she knew either brother. The disgust of that nasty deed done just to get money for drugs soured in his throat. A murder and a rape: just two of the many evils he had done, and those only pertained to two people in the room. There were scores, hundreds, more of them. It would take years of his life to track down everyone he had wronged and apologize, but he could start right now, here. By giving his father the same compassion he sought from others, he would be helping both of them heal.

"Okay," Van said, rising to stand on the other side of

Quinn. "I forgive you. I have to ask, though; you're not having any more children, are you?"

Quinn froze and Charles looked around like he had missed something. "No. Do you know something I don't?"

"No," Van said, and bent down to shake the man's hand. "Just wanted to make sure."

Junior coughed, trying to get Van's attention. Van looked his way and saw Junior cut his eyes over to Missy Lou, sitting on her mother's lap. Cindy grinned, seeing the intent.

"Oh, and by the way," Van said, adding a wink up at Quinn. "You're a grandpa. I know, it's a lot to take in, finding out you have another son, all of the sudden. But that son is married and has a wife...and they have a daughter."

Cindy had risen at the introduction and was squatted in front of Charles by the end of the declaration. "Say hi to your Grandpa, Missy Lou."

"And watch her grasp!" Junior warned. "She's got the fastest hands in the west."

Everyone in the room watched as Cindy gently set her daughter on Charles's knee. "Say, Grandpa," she encouraged.

The room was silent, waiting for her first greeting.

Thud, thud, thud....

Even the baby looked up and followed the sound of footfalls on the roof.

"Santa?" Butch whispered.

But O'Reilly was cautious. He stood up, gun drawn, and followed the footfalls toward the chimney.

"Hey, Vinny," a voice called. "It got quiet down there all of the sud..."

Crash!

Thunk! Thunk!

A three-foot section of the roof caved in. One, then two men in dark suits fell through the opening, the larger of the two on the bottom. The one on top scrambled for his gun, then realized there were three guns drawn on him.

"Merry Christmas?" he said weakly and rolled off the man

beneath him.

The one remaining on the floor lifted up his upper body, looking like a very fat cobra, and said, "Yeah. Ho, ho, ho," then fell forward, his bandaged hand pointed skyward.

"Vinny the Axe and Hugo," Quinn said, shaking his head. "Idiots."

"I got this," O'Reilly said, nodding to Quinn and Pete who both had their weapons drawn. "Van, do you want to do the honors since it was probably you they were after?"

"Oh, yeah. Give me the zip ties."

"I'll take the one on the bottom," Junior said. "I can't let you have all the fun, especially since they were after me before they knew you were hanging around, too."

"Grandpa!" Missy Lou squealed, clutching her newly acknowledged grandfather's nose.

Van and Junior momentarily looked her way, and Vinny reached for his gun again.

"Oh, just give me a reason to decorate the halls with bits of you," Quinn said, then looked to make sure that O'Reilly had a bead drawn on him, too. "And believe me, I will not shoot to kill. I can't wait to hear they've sent you to prison. You think you have enemies on the outside, the guys on the inside are going to have so much fun with you."

"Eh, eh, eh," Van chastised. "Junior and I will bind them up, then the sheriff can put them in the back of his rig until dinner's done."

"And Mama still has to read us the story of Peter Elph. I know it's your first Christmas with us, big brother, but one thing you're going to love about being in this family is tradition. You've been around for so few of them. We still have lots more to share with you."

"Can we stay?" Charles asked, Missy Lou's clutch now released, her head laying comfortably on his shoulder.

"Plenty of food for everyone...except for maybe the riff-raff," Pete said. Loretta nudged him in the ribs again. "Even the riff-raff. It'll probably be the last real food they'll see for twenty to life, anyhow."

Chapter 7: The Wagner Legacy

After Christmas Eve dinner

"Are you sure we should head back tonight?" Butch asked, looking out the window. "We got the roof tarped and it's nice and dry inside. The snow's really coming down hard now. I don't want to get stuck in it."

"You're all welcome to stay, 'ceptin maybe the riff-raff," Pete said, then glared at the two men who had shared the last piece of pecan pie, robbing him of his second one.

"I guess they can stay in the back of the rig," O'Reilly said, frowning in indecision.

"Are you sure you want to put them out there?" Junior asked. "You'd have to leave the heater and engine running all night or they'd freeze to death."

Hugo gasped in sudden fear. Vinny shoved his shoulder into his, letting him know to be silent.

"That'd suck up a lot of gas," Pete said to the sheriff. "Would you have enough for the return trip if you did? Maybe it'd be best if you didn't run the heater." He paused, then added with a wink, "I'm just messin' with you."

"Oh, I don't know," O'Reilly said, enjoying the panic the scared contract killers were showing.

"Hey, I got an idea," Pete said. "Why don't you put a rope around their necks or something so they'll choke if they try to run? And maybe see if you can figure out how to secure them to the washing machine or something else that's too heavy to run away with."

"Where would they go?" O'Reilly said. "They'd freeze to death before they reached the main road."

Another gasp from Hugo and shove from Vinny made

Quinn chuckle. "I'm pretty good at tying knots. I was an Eagle Scout. Got any rope around here? I can make sure we're all doubly safe."

"I'm on it," Pete said. He grabbed his coat from the series of hooks on the wall by the door, slipped on his boots, and headed to the barn.

"Yeah, stay the night," O'Reilly said, his head bobbing in conviction as he thought more about it. "Looks like it's a good thing there's plenty of blankets. It's gonna be toeses to noses, though."

"Everyone ready for storytime?" Cecelia asked, trying to break up the criminal-tainted atmosphere with some Christmas spirit.

"Nope," Loretta said. "You're not starting without my Pete."

"Oh, so it's 'my Pete' now?" she asked.

"Yup. I let him claim me last night," Loretta said, her face aglow.

"Mom!" Cindy, Van, and Junior exclaimed.

"Well, it's about time!" Cecelia said. She leaned over to her sister and asked, "Well, did you like it?"

"Oh, yeah. Worth waiting fifty years for."

Junior and Van shuffled chairs and footstools around while Quinn used a borrowed blanket to make sure Charles's legs and feet were covered.

Stomp! Stomp! Stomp!

Pete walked in the front door, brandishing the coil of rope like it was a twenty-pound catfish. "Look what I got? A peaceful night's sleep." He toe-to-heel removed his boots, then hung up his coat. "Will this work?" he asked Quinn, bringing it over to him.

Quinn unwound one end, set the round into the crook of his elbow, and tugged on a one-foot length. "Yup, good braided nylon rope. I can make a slip knot that'll remind them not to turn over or even scratch their balls in their sleep." He looked over at the hand-covered grins on Lucy and Cindy. "Sorry about that, ladies," he said. "That was crude. I guess I wasn't thinking."

"No, don't worry about us, right?" Cindy looked at her two mothers and Lucy.

"All men's got 'em," Cecelia said, "and they're bound to itch at some time or another."

"Hey, Grandpa," Butch said to O'Reilly. He nodded at Cecelia. "Can we keep her? She's funny. I like her. A lot."

Cecelia stepped over and gave the high school senior a big hug. "I think he'd have to work real hard to get rid of me."

O'Reilly put an arm around each of them and pulled them close. "I'm not letting either of you go. At least, for a year."

"Huh?" Butch asked, but Cecelia only smiled.

"You graduate this summer," Cecelia said. "I think he figures you're going to college or trade school or maybe get an internship..."

"Nope. If anything, I'm getting a local job or maybe going to community college. I want to have a mother for a while. It's been too long without one."

Sniff. Sniff.

All heads turned toward the sound of barely contained weeping. "Are you all right?" Quinn asked, then realized he was with family and added, "Dear."

"I can't believe how much I messed up with Van. God, I'm so glad you," he said, looking at Cecelia, "and Loretta — that's your name, right? — adopted him. Having a mother... Scratch that. Having a loving mother and father, or grandfather..."

"Parent?" Quinn suggested.

"Yes. Being a loving parent and spending time with your child is worth more than traveling to Singapore to seal a merger or having the classiest yacht in the Sydney Regatta. What was I thinking?"

"Charles, your father was rich and powerful, right?" Quinn asked, his hand gentle on his shoulder.

Charles sniffed and nodded. "So, you think that's why I was the same way?"

"Children, dogs, critters — two and four-legged — all learn from their parents or elders or whoever is in charge," Pete said.

"Looks like Van's a smart one. He broke the cycle on his own."

"More or less," Van said and shrugged. "A lot got broken on the way, not just the cycle," and rolled his eyes in exasperation. He pulled off a length of paper towels and handed it to his father. "You'll get there, too. Baby steps, Dad. At least for this part of your life, you have a good helper. Or partner or whatever."

Charles reached up and patted Quinn's hand on his. "Partner and more."

"Okay, everyone," Cecelia said. "Enough of this sappy stuff. Now it's time for a scoop of history served in a bowl of tradition."

"Yum," Hugo said, then, "Oof," as Vinny thumped him with his head. "Sorry," he said softly. "I can't help that I like food."

"What's your name?" Cecelia asked, although she knew he had already been read his rights and didn't have to answer.

"Hugo Cotella," he said, then gasped and ducked sideways, averting another angry nudge from the man tied to him.

"Idiot!" Vinny screeched.

"Do. Not. Call. Me. That!" Hugo enunciated. He waited, knowing that Vinny would make another comment. As soon as Vinny turned to him with mouth open — probably to apologize for saying that trigger word — Hugo flipped his head back and let him have it.

Thunk!

"Ah, shit, Hugo. I think you broke my dose again," Vinny said, blood flowing down his chin.

"Good. Hey, Sheriff. Can you make sure we don't get put in the same cell when we get wherever we're going? I don't never want to see this goon again."

"I'll do my best," O'Reilly said, chewing back the chuckle. He pulled out another length of paper towels, looked at it, then grabbed another couple feet and stuffed it under Vinny's chin. "Now, it's time for what my dear Cecelia tells me is part of the Wagner family tradition. The story of Peter Elph has been handed down orally through the generations. Last year, she put it together in a book so others, as in non-Wagner friends or family, can enjoy the story of the little boy reunited with his father."

Sniff! Sniff!

"Don't worry," Quinn said, hugging Charles's head to his shoulder. "We got this."

Cecelia read the story, her inflections and tones rising and lowering to capture the voices of the different characters: young Peter Elph, the evil banker out to steal and destroy, and all the others in 1886 Tombstone.

"Were they real?" Hugo asked.

"Yes, they were," Loretta said, her hand holding Pete's. "At least, that's what our parents told us, and their parents told them, and so on; all the way back to the silver mining days of old Arizona."

"And," Cecelia said, drawing out the suspense. She set a one-foot-square box on her lap and pulled off the lid. "And here's the little wooden horse that Peter carved for his son. See," she turned it upside down and showed off the carved initials, "P.W. 1886. Peter Wagner."

Charles straightened up in the chair and cleared his throat. "That's a very interesting story, Ms. Wagner, but all's well now. Van can go back to being a Van der Cleft."

"No offense," Van said, forgoing the title dad or father that he had used when he was younger, depending on whether he was asking for something or was angry. "But I think I'll stick with the name Wagner. Pretty cool legacy: Tombstone gambler and Arabian horses, eh, Mama, Mom?"

Charles's eyes filled with tears. "I don't know whether to be happy or sad. I'm glad you made a wise decision, choosing grace and kindness over money, but I'm also sad. I'm losing a son."

"Nah. I'll stick around, just in case you need a kidney or something. But since there are still some assassins out there looking for me and/or my brother, can we keep this just between us? That is, you and Quinn," he added with a wink, "and the rest of my family."

Quinn walked up and put his hand on Van's shoulder. "You grew up to be a man. Scratch that, a true gentleman, despite the hardships of entitlement." He paused, a frown twitching on his handsome face. "That sounds odd. Wrong. The hardships of entitlement..."

"Yeah, well, it's true," Van said. "Look how everyone turned out. I had two parents, but I'm a wreck."

"Were a wreck," Lucy interjected, then said, "Sorry. Go ahead."

"I was a wreck with the 'perfect' parents, home, plenty of money, the best education money could buy. At least, it would have been if I had paid attention. But Lucy was reared by a single parent and she's an absolute angel."

Lucy leaned in and kissed him on the cheek, then sat back, more radiant than ever.

"And Junior didn't even have a father figure. Both he and Cindy were brought up by two mothers. Both turned out to be very classy people in my book."

Cindy nodded to Quinn and Charles. "And just for the record, my mothers *were* lesbians. Gender identification has absolutely nothing to do with anything. I just wish you had come to your senses earlier. Looks to me like it's time to claim Quinn as your own and kick that wannabe child assassin out of the nest."

"Can I help?" Hugo said, sitting up straight. "If I let the judge know she's the one that hired us to kill Van, do you think they'll let me off easy?"

The sheriff looked at Quinn and Charles, then at Vinny, then back at Hugo. "You'd do that? You know, I did read you your rights. You don't have a lawyer here, so anything you say probably won't be admissible in court."

"I can be his lawyer," Lucy said, waving her hand in the air. "I'm not a lawyer yet, but I can be his advocate without a degree. Hugo, I'm asking you before everyone in this room, do you want me to be your advocate? That's like your lawyer, but I won't charge you a whole bunch."

"Yeah. Sounds good to me."

"Okay. Before witnesses you have your lawyer. Now, that's enough business for a Christmas Eve celebration. Anyone else have any surprises?"

Van raised his hand and grinned.

"Only good news allowed in my house tonight," Pete said.

Van looked over at Quinn and his father, a happy family unit, snuggled around Missy Lou, napping on her grandpa's chest. "You're going to have to start working out, Dad," he said with a wink.

"Oh, we're already on the health kick," Quinn said. "He's getting better every day, and it's only been four days."

"Why do you say that, son?" Charles asked.

"Because you're going to need a broader chest and stronger arms. I don't know if you noticed, but little Missy Lou's mother is going to have another baby soon."

Charles looked over at Cindy. She turned sideways and showed off her baby bump with a smile. "I thought she just was a big girl. Two grandchildren? Marvelous!" he said, tears of joy trickling out the side of his eyes.

"And then..." Van said, waiting for the little chatter of remarks to die down.

Charles sniffed back the tears. "Yes, son. And then..." he prompted.

"Lucy and I will give you a grandchild."

"Or two," Lucy said, nodding to Cecelia.

"Yup," Cecelia confirmed. "I have a bit of experience with delivering twins, so we're all set."

Thunk!

"Van!" Lucy screeched, then started laughing when she saw him wink. "You imp!"

"Actually," he admitted, "I did lose my legs for a second but controlled the fall. See, Dad," he said, looking to Charles, "there's no way I'd leave my real family."

"Yes, your 'real' family is priceless."

"Your lost and found family," Quinn said, the strength of conviction in his simple declaration. "Sometimes it takes a while to find who you're truly supposed to be with." He patted Charles on the shoulder. "Once you find them, never give up, never let go."

The End

CPSIA information can be obtained
at www.ICGtesting.com
Printed in the USA
BVHW060730090123
655879BV00014B/873

9 781806 304271